The Night Heroes:

The Blade of Black Crow

By
Dr. Bo Wagner

Word of His Mouth Publishers
Mooresboro, NC

All Scripture quotations are taken from the **King James Version** of the Bible.

ISBN: 978-1-941039-91-5
Printed in the United States of America
© 2014 Dr. Bo Wagner (Robert Arthur Wagner)

Word of His Mouth Publishers
Mooresboro, NC
www.wordofhismouth.com

Chapter One

It should come as no surprise that the entire cabin of our Yukon smelled like chicken and fries and sounded like the cacophony of a state fair. As we left Rossville, Georgia, dad (of course) swung us through the Bojangles drive through. He and mom were chowing down on their Cajun Fillet combos, I was scarfing down a steak biscuit, and my two sisters, Carrie and Aly, had chicken tenders biscuits and fries.

In between bites was the cacophony. Anytime the five of us are confined to a small area, it gets very noisy. A happy kind of noisy, but noisy nonetheless. Raven-haired Carrie, age twelve, was pontificating upon Legolas the elf and why he was better than normal boys. Dad is fine with that. Normal boys, no, imaginary elves, yes.

Bubbly blonde-haired Aly, age eleven, was singing. She was always singing. On this particular day she was singing a hilarious Tim Hawkins song, "The Dog's on Fire."

In between my bites I was nicely fussing at them, trying to get them to be quite. My head was hurting from our last adventure, and I really could have used some quiet. Dad always says my arms are stronger than my head. I am not sure if that is a compliment or an insult, but knowing dad, it is probably a bit of both.

I suppose that, whoever you are, you might not know who we are. If that is the case, it means that you have not read any of our other books telling about our other adventures! You'll definitely have to fix that, but for now, let me quickly get you up to speed.

We, me and my two sisters, the Warner kids, are the Night Heroes.

My dad is an evangelist, which means that he travels around all over the place preaching. We have done that with him for years, and up until a few months ago we were just like everybody else. But on a trip to West

Virginia something unusual happened. We heard a voice calling our names in the middle of the night, and when we woke up, it wasn't night anymore. It also wasn't our present day! We had somehow been transported back in time to the coal mines of 1912. The Conductor of the train told us that the Lord had called for us to rescue a little boy whom some very bad men had trapped in the coal mine. We would be awake during the day in our time, he explained, and then when we went to sleep we would wake up in the past.

We would try, during the time we were awake in the past, to get the job done, and then at night when we went to sleep, providing we were not being held captive somewhere, we would wake back up in our time and feel just as rested as if we had gotten a full night's sleep. We had five days, and five days only, to do the job.

We learned that if we were injured in any way, we would wake up with that injury. We also discovered that whatever we went to sleep with, we carried with us into the past. That was very helpful!

Well, we did rescue that little boy, but that turned out to be just the beginning of our adventures. While at a meeting in Fayetteville,

North Carolina, home of the world famous 82nd airborne, we found ourselves having a night time adventure in Nazi Germany of World War II. We managed to rescue a little girl named Miriam from the Ravensbruck Concentration Camp.

Last week we were in Rossville, Georgia, with Pastor Ricky Gravley and the Bible Baptist Church. That is right outside the Chickamauga Battlefield, and sure enough we found ourselves in an adventure right in the middle of the Civil War, during the Battle of Chickamauga.

Now you know why my head was hurting.

Dad is not exactly the sympathetic type, though. His favorite phrase, at least to use on me, is, "Hey, Kyle, suck it up, buttercup."

I know he is just trying to make sure I grow up tough and strong. He is doing a good job with that. Despite our travels, he makes sure that I work very hard and work out very hard. I may be fourteen, but I am really strong! A bad man in the mines of West Virginia found that out the hard way when I cracked his jaw for him.

Carrie is the brainiac of our team. I really believe she could embarrass Einstein if she wanted to. Common sense? Uh, no. Genius? Yeah, definitely.

Aly is the spark plug. She is a pint-sized, lightning-in-a-bottle kind of a person. She is unpredictable, absolutely fearless, and a bit moody.

That's us, the Night Heroes.

At the moment we were driving from Georgia toward Tennessee. Rogersville, Tennessee, to be exact. Three hours, one hundred eighty-four miles. Dad was going to be preaching for a really great preacher named Barry Rackley, at the Rogersville Baptist Temple. Dad says that Brother Rackley is one of the best preachers of our generation.

One hundred eighty-four miles is no big deal for us, we are used to that kind of traveling. Still, it was really nice to see the signs for Rogersville as we came up I-81. We got off at exit 23, and a bit later (And yes, Aly got carsick on the winding roads. Again.) we got to the Comfort Inn in Rogersville. It was around 4:35, and we quickly checked in to room 203.

As always, we knew exactly what we needed to do even without being told. After growing up on the road, everyone knew exactly what to carry in out of the vehicle, who would sleep where, who got the bathroom first (Mom and the girls, every single time) and what we needed to do to get ready for church.

By 6:10 we were ready and out the door. We turned left out of the parking lot, followed the drive on down to Burton Road, took a right, and almost immediately pulled into the parking lot of Rogersville Baptist Temple.

The church is really pretty, mid-sized, and the folks there were doing some nice renovations to the sanctuary. But as always, the best part of any church is the people, not the building. All of the people there were really, really friendly! We especially liked Mrs. Elisha, Pastor Rackley's wife.

At seven sharp the service started. The choir really did an awesome job, there were some great specials, and the entire atmosphere in the place was really good!

Finally it was time for the best part of any service, the preaching. I really like my dad's preaching; lots of people do. Dad preached a message he preaches almost everywhere, Choosing Your Final Destination. Just like last week, someone came and accepted Christ as Savior during the invitation. This time it was a great little nine-year-old boy named Blake. I love that; I just love it!

In a way, I wish that every service would last forever. But on the other hand, the first night of any meeting always makes me a little tired, especially after a long drive. I guess mom and dad know that, because as soon as the service was over we went to Wendy's with Pastor Rackley and then straight back to the hotel.

We got ready for bed, prayed together, everyone hugged everyone else, and it was time for lights out.

And for lying there in the dark wondering.

We never knew, really, when we would be called to a mission and when we would have an uneventful week. Some weeks no call in the night came, and nothing at all happened. Other weeks the call did come, and we ended up on a train, or a plane, or in a wagon, desperately trying to help someone in need. I knew Carrie and Aly, tired as they were, were also lying awake in the dark wondering the same thing I was.

Or so I thought.

When I heard their soft snores, I knew better. Brats! Here I was lying awake, and they were already sawing logs.

I'm really not sure why that bugged me, but for some reason it did. So, with a "harumph," I rolled over and joined them in a peaceful sleep.

Chapter Two

At some point during the night I began to shiver. I could feel a cold breeze blowing across my face, and I could smell the strong but lovely scent of pine. Somewhere in my head I could also make out the sound of running water, like a creek burbling across rocks, winding its way down, down, down into a deep valley somewhere.

The voice, when it came, was in a whisper, a very urgent whisper.

"Kyle! Kyle!"

Something in me froze, yet snapped wide awake. I wasn't sure why, but for some reason I sensed imminent danger.

A couple of years ago I picked up one of my dad's Louis L'Amour books, an old western. I was immediately hooked, and from then on scarfed up as many of them as I could find. That being the case, I knew what I needed to do.

Without moving my body at all, I rolled my eyes to my right and saw a deep dark forest falling away from me. I could hear the river to that side, and I knew that was the source of the water I heard earlier.

But the whisper had come from my left. I rolled my eyes back that way, and saw three sets of eyes peering out from behind a huge old fir tree. The lowest set of eyes belonged to Aly, and her eyes registered panic. That worried me. A lot. The next set of eyes up were the dark brown eyes of Carrie, and hers showed urgency, which I figure is just a more composed form of panic. The highest set of eyes were those that I had come to know over the last few months as those of the Conductor, whom we had first met on that old train in West Virginia. His eyes showed no panic, but they were sending me an unmistakable message: be very, very careful!

Quickly I scanned my surroundings from my lying position. It was clearly very early in the morning, just before sunrise. The fir tree behind which my sisters and the Conductor were for some reason taking refuge was about ten feet away. From the fir tree the ground sloped upward for a very long way, so I judged that I was on a path midway up some mountainside.

Seeing nothing, but knowing that there had to be a reason why everyone was whispering for me so urgently, I cautiously rolled over onto my stomach, and then eased up onto my knees.

I looked over again at the tree and saw the Conductor motioning for me to stay low. So I rose up onto my feet, but stayed hunched over, and began to slowly take one step after another toward the tree.

Apparently, that was not low enough.

"DOWN!"

That came from the Conductor, and it came in a scream.

I immediately dropped flat onto my stomach, and as I was dropping I heard a "whoosh" come by my right ear, and then I heard a "thunk" from the fir tree.

As quick as a flash I was crawling like a soldier in boot camp, racing for the tree. As

I got to it then behind it, I heard another "whoosh, thunk!"

"Arrows!" from Aly and, "Indians!" from Carrie and, "Run!" from the Conductor hit my ears all at the same time.

And boy, did we ever run! We went uphill since the arrows had come from below us, and without even having to be told we zigged and zagged from tree to tree, not wanting whoever it was to get a clear shot at us. There were at least five or six more "whoosh, thunks" before they finally stopped.

But we did not stop. We ran like scared rabbits, always uphill, and as far as I knew none of us other than the Conductor had any idea what was going on. This was definitely different! In our previous three missions we had the chance to get acclimated, up to speed with what was going on and what was expected of us, and then we got to choose the time, place, and manner in which we entered our danger zone. This time the danger had come first, and for all I knew we weren't going to live long enough to figure out what in the world was happening, or when in the world it was happening!

After maybe five minutes of hard chugging uphill, we spotted a dark opening in the face of the mountain, the opening to a cave. Without so much as an ounce of discussion we all dove in through the entrance of the cave, rolled over several times, and came to a stop in the darkness. The just occurring sunrise was not casting any rays into that cave; indeed, from the way it was facing I knew that the cave had never seen any light unless it was from the light of a fire.

We lay there on our backs for a while, trying desperately to catch our breath and compose ourselves. Finally, the Conductor broke the silence.

"Welcome once again, Night Heroes. My apologies for such an abrupt entry into your newest mission. It was certainly not my intention for things to begin this way."

Laying there in the darkness, hearing him but not able to see his face, I pondered for maybe the first time ever on his accent. It was not exactly British, but it certainly wasn't standard   South-of-the-Mason-Dixon-Line English either. In fact, it really didn't sound at all like any other accent from anywhere I knew.

It was Carrie that broke my train of musing.

"It's no problem, sir, no problem at all. But whoever was shooting at us certainly intended to make a point..."

She dragged out that last line, the way she always does when she is making a pun. She picked that habit up from our dad, who is always saying something corny too.

"Oh, har har, big sis, that was really cute," Aly chimed in with obvious sarcasm. "But why don't you refrain from practicing your hopeless humor long enough for us to let the Conductor tell us exactly what is going on, and why someone is already trying to kill us!"

"Fair enough, pipsqueak," Carrie said with a smile in her voice, "I'll quit, honest Injun!"

Even the Conductor groaned at that one.

"Aly is right, Night Heroes, I do need to let you know what is happening and what you are needed for. Why don't we start the way we started last time? Carrie, do you think you can figure out roughly when and where you are?"

In case you don't know, Carrie, our resident genius, has the knack for noticing everything, and making some pretty logical deductions based on what she sees.

"Well," she began slowly, "the arrows are a pretty good indication that we are in a far earlier time than we have ever been to before, most likely somewhere in the seventeen hundreds. I doubt if we are as far back as the sixteen hundreds, because whoever that Indian was shot at us on sight. For there to be that kind of animosity against not just white man, but white *children,* you would have to be past the sixteen hundreds, and on up into the time when there started being serious battles over land and resources.

"As to the place, I am guessing we are still in Tennessee, somewhere in the general vicinity of what will one day be Rogersville. The types of trees we passed while running up here are all native to the mountains of Tennessee, and the Tennessee Valley area was a huge hotbed of Indian activity. In fact, I seem to remember that Davy Crockett's grandparents were killed in an Indian massacre in or near Rogersville."

The growing light outside of the cave, and my eyes getting better adjusted, allowed me to make out a big smile on the Conductor's face.

"As always, Carrie, your powers of observation and logical deduction are impeccable, as is your memory of your studies. You are indeed still in the mountains of

Tennessee, not too many miles from what will one day be Rogersville. And it is, in fact, the late seventeen hundreds, 1778 to be exact. That year is significant. Today is exactly one year to the day since David Crockett and his wife, the grandparents of Davy Crockett, were killed.

"Since that massacre one year ago, much blood has been shed on both sides. A bitter hatred has taken root, and many more lives are likely to be lost in the next few years. But as before, your concern is much more individualized.

"For more than fifty years now, Bible-believing Christians have done their best to spread the gospel to the natives of this new land and to their own people of the white race. They have been successful in seeing many souls won to Christ. One family in particular became Christians some years ago, a man, his wife, and their now twelve-year-old son. The mother was killed in an attack shortly thereafter, and the father, who was left for dead, survived but is paralyzed from the waist down.

"Their son, a godly boy named Samuel, was out in the field working a few days ago and was taken by some marauding Creek Indians. The chief of that tribe is dying, and his son, Black Crow, wants more than anything in the world to be the new chief. His younger son, Falling Rain, would be a wise and compassionate chief and would be able to bring a halt to much of the hatred and bloodshed between his tribe and the settlers. But Black Crow becoming chief would mean much more war and much more bloodshed."

"Excuse me for asking, sir," I interjected, "but what does Samuel have to do with any of that?"

"Good question, Kyle. What it has to do with all of this is that Black Crow intends to use Samuel as a demonstration of his strength and ruthlessness. He has called the tribe to a meeting the Friday night of the full moon, five days from now. At that time he has stated that he will 'kill the fierce white warrior,' thus proving that he is the wisest choice to be the new chief."

"Let me guess," Aly piped in, "the 'fierce white warrior' is Samuel, right?"

"Correct, Aly, correct. Now, the truth is, Samuel is just an ordinary boy, there is really nothing fierce or war-like about him. If he has to face Black Crow, he will be killed, and he knows it. And so he has done what he has learned from Scripture; he has called out to the Lord for help just as Daniel and the three

Hebrew boys did so long, long ago. Like them, he is not afraid to die, but he also, like all of you, has no desire to do so if it can be avoided!"

I could not help but notice that he said "all of you" instead of "all of us." I had already decided on our second mission that he must be an angel, or at least some kind of heavenly being. Whatever he was, it was always good to have him around, even though the mission itself was our responsibility.

"And we are here to make sure he doesn't die, is that right?" said Aly.

"It is, young lady, it is. How you do that is up to you, but, as always, you have only five days to get the job done. Once your father's revival meeting is over, you will not be coming back to this time."

"We understand, sir, we understand," I said seriously. "And as always, we will either get the job done, or at least give it everything in our power to do so."

"All that is fine and good," Carrie chimed in, "but have we forgotten one little monkey wrench in the machinery? We are in a cave, and for all we know whatever Indian was shooting at us is still out there just waiting for one of us to poke our heads out so he can put an arrow into it. How are we going to rescue

Samuel while trapped in a cave, and how are we going to get out of the cave without risking getting shot?"

Chapter Three

I had to admit that was a very good question. I, for one, did not need any more holes in my head. Nor did my sisters, although they probably had more brain cells to spare than I did.

"What do you think, Mr. Conductor?" I said as I turned back to him. But when I did, I got the shock of my life–he wasn't there!

Carrie and Aly whirled around 360 degrees in a circle, looking all around the parts of the cave where the Conductor had just been standing. But he absolutely was not there.

"Wow," Aly said slowly, "this isn't at all starting off like our other missions."

"No," I said, "not exactly. But we all know that our Conductor is just our transportation and guide to our mission. What we do is up to us; he does not get involved any more than he has to. That's okay, though; we're not exactly new to tight situations."

"No, I suppose not," said Carrie. "Still, I'm not sure exactly how we're going to manage to get out of this one."

"Well, there are two directions to go in a cave," Aly chirped, "and since out is not a good option, why don't we try in?"

And with that, she pulled a little LED flashlight out of her pocket, clicked it on, and twirled it around like a light saber.

"Ow, Sis, you need to stop," I said, "before we all get a headache. But your idea may just be a good one if this cave is anything at all like the one we just saw at Ruby Falls. Do you remember? Down in the lower cave water ran out into the river, and up through the rocks there were places for the smoke from the fires lit in the cave to escape. Most caves have other ways to get in and out, providing you don't get stuck in a nook or cranny and die, I mean."

"Oh that's comforting, big brother, real comforting," Carrie drawled.

I couldn't let that go unanswered.

"Do you have a better idea, brainiac?"

"As a matter of fact I do," she said somewhat smugly. "Let's throw a line out and see if any fish out there bites. Let me see your jacket. And, Aly, do you have that bandana you usually carry around with you in your pack?"

"Uh, sure, but where in the world are you going with this?"

"Just trust me," she said, "I have a plan. Kyle, ball up your jacket into something about the size of a head. In the meantime, let me fish around in my stuff for some lip gloss and a marker,"

Now that caught me off guard!

"Um, Sis," I said as I balled up my jacket and handed it to her, "what in the world are you up to?"

"I'm going to give our arrow-happy buddy out there a target," she said as she went to work. "If he is still out there, I figure he is sitting there with hand to string, just tensed up and waiting for someone to stick a head out. If he is, I don't think he's going to be too picky who or what he shoots at. There!" she said as she turned my jacket around for us to see, "I think that looks a lot like you!"

Oh, she was going to pay for that! I was now staring at a grotesque cotton face, with glossy lips and magic marker drawn eyes and a crooked, gap-toothed smile!

"You...will...pay for this, somehow, some way," I said.

"Yeah, yeah, yeah, whatever. Let's just get this thing mounted and ready. Anyone got anything like a stick?"

"A stick?" I said incredulously. "No, Sis, I don't usually carry those to bed with me. There are no doubt plenty of them just outside the cave, if you want to go grab one, but I wouldn't recommend it. What about you, Aly, did you take a stick to bed with you in your pack?"

"Nope, sorry, no stick. Not unless you count my chopsticks, I mean."

Yeah, jaw dropping moment, that one. I looked over at Carrie, and she looked back over at me, and we both said it about the same time, "Why in the world did you put chopsticks in your night pack?!?"

"Hey, we've been to the coal war of 1912, Germany, and Chickamauga. Eventually we are going to end up somewhere where they serve old timey Chinese or Japanese food, and I am going to be ready when that happens."

"Sis," I said as I put my hands on her tiny shoulders, "you are as weird as a three and a half dollar bill, but I love you. Don't ever be normal; it just wouldn't be you. Let me borrow one of those chopsticks."

A minute or so later we had our head mounted on a tiny stick. It would only give me a ten inch handle or so, but that should be enough for me to stick the fake head far enough out of the cave to avoid getting an arrow shot through my hand. I slipped up to the edge of the cave, and about head high stuck the head out sideways as if a person was peering around the corner.

Nothing.

I turned around and said, "Looks like good news, Sis, no Ind..."

I had not even finished the word before it happened. With a "whoosh, whap!" the fake head was ripped off of the chopstick and out of my hand, and landed somewhere in the back of the cave! I nearly jumped out of my skin!

I stood there shaking for a minute, then turned to the girls, and we all said it at once, "Out is out of the question!"

Chapter Four

The cave was nowhere near as big as the coal mine in our first adventure, nor was it as open and smooth as the one that led to Ruby Falls when we were in Chickamauga. The only spot that had any real space to it was the very opening part where we had taken refuge. As we made our way back into the confines, it grew narrower and narrower. Aly's little LED light worked like a champ, and we were able to see well in whatever direction I aimed it.

We had woven our way back into it maybe a hundred yards or so when things got really, really tight.

"Whew, guys, it's really narrow up here. I won't be able to go straight ahead; I'll have to see if I can wiggle my way sideways."

I turned to the side and just barely managed to squeeze my way further ahead. Behind me, Aly and Carry did the same, and we made good progress for maybe another fifty yards or so, until the unthinkable happened.

"Um, guys, I'm stuck!"

I said the words calmly, but I could feel a tinge of fear rising up in my chest. Looking ahead, I realized that things only got narrower. There would be no going further ahead. Back was our only option.

"Ok, here's the deal. As much as I hate to say it, we're gonna have to go back. You two are going to have to grab my hand and pull me back that way, and then we'll make our way back to the entry of the cave and figure something out."

I handed them the flashlight, then Carrie grabbed my hand, Aly grabbed hers, and on the count of three they tugged with all of their might, and I lunged toward them. And with all of that concerted effort, I went absolutely nowhere! Now I could really feel the panic setting in.

"Pull harder, guys, lots harder!"

They yanked again, and I mean they pulled hard enough that my shoulder hurt. But it didn't help, not even a little. I was absolutely stuck fast.

"Kyle, we have a problem," Carrie said calmly. "That's all we've got. We can't pull you out; we are going to have to think you out."

"Think me out? THINK me out?!? What is this, Sis, some kind of a New Age Yoga rescue? I don't want to be thought out; I want to be pulled out!"

"SHUSH!" Carrie exploded. And I shushed.

"That's better. I'm not talking about anything New Age or mystical; we've all been taught better than that. What I'm saying is, we need to use the strongest muscle in our bodies."

I knew what she meant. Dad, the strongest man I know, always says, "And now, watch me use the strongest muscle in my body," right before he does something incredibly smart. He can lift hundreds of pounds, but his first option is always to think of leverage, or angles, or something to make things as efficient as possible. "God has given us these wonderful things called brains," he says, "and when we do not use them, we dishonor Him."

"Ok, Sis, let's use those brains, then."

"Good," she said with what sounded like a smile on her face. "Now, let's think in terms of directions. Is forward an option?"

"Clearly not," I said flatly.

"Ok, forward is not an option, and we have already tried backward," she said slowly, "how about down? Can you scooch down and wiggle your way out?"

For the record, "scooch" is, as far as I can tell, a distinctly southern word. But since I understood it, I figured I would try and find out. I exhaled and tried to wiggle my way down to the ground.

"Nothing doing, Sis," I said, "I can make it an inch or two and that's it."

"Ok, then how about the only other direction? How about up?"

I must admit, that had not at all occurred to me.

"Aly, shine your flashlight up over my head and let me see what it looks like."

Immediately the area over my head was bathed with white light. All three of us looked up, and gasped at the exact same time. For there, over my head, was a natural shaft, a cleft in the rock, weaving upward like a snake. It appeared to be wider than where we were presently standing and squirming. If I were able to pull myself free, and up, we could get out of this mess, and maybe even find another way out.

"Ok, guys, now would be a good time to pray for me. There is a ledge just over my head, and I should be able to reach it with my hands. If I am strong enough, I may be able to pull myself free."

With that, I reached up and, sure enough, was able to get my fingers over the edge of that ledge. This would be a pull-up kind of move, which fortunately my dad has already had me doing to improve my strength. I breathed in and out a few times, and then pulled as hard as I could pull. For the first second or two, nothing, and then I started to move.

"C'mon, Kyle, PULL!" Aly shouted. And I did. More and more, higher and higher, till finally I practically shot upward.

"Yes! Yes! Here we go."

I angled my body so that I could get a foot onto the side of the rock where a few seconds ago my hands had been. Getting that into place, I used my right leg to push even further upward, and into an area where I could brace between the walls of the cleft and sit still and breathe for a moment. Then I looked back down, into Aly's light."

"Ow, Sis, how about shining that off to the side a bit?"

"Sorry, Bro," she said."

"No problem. Hand me that light up here for a minute."

Aly handed the light to Carrie, and Carrie handed it up to me. I held it up and looked overhead and around with it.

"Hey, guys, I have no idea where it goes, but this rift in the rock goes up and then angles forward."

"Well, it's about the only option we have at this point, I would think," Carrie said with a giggle.

"Yeah, I would say so. Do you two think you can climb up after me?"

"Don't make me hurt you, Kyle, and don't make me embarrass you either," Aly snapped. "The only real question is, do I climb past you and leave you, or do I hang around for your slow self?"

"Touché, Sis, touché."

And with that we begin to climb. I held the flashlight in my mouth, because for the most part each and every foot of progress required the use of both hands and both feet.

The girls stayed right on my heels, never missing a beat.

After what seemed like forever, I stopped.

"Hey, do you guys notice something?"

"Other than the fact that your feet stink?"

"Cute, Carrie, real cute. I'm serious. Take a deep sniff of the air."

I could hear two noses below me inhaling, and almost immediately Aly said, "It smells cleaner and fresher than it has been."

"Exactly. That means that somewhere ahead or above, there is an opening to the outside. If we find it, and if it is big enough, we can get out!"

"And if it isn't?" Carrie asked.

"It has to be, Sis, because the only other two options are to stay here forever, or fall back down into the main shaft of the cave."

"Gotcha. Opening. Find it, and pray that it is big enough."

We struggled on, mostly following my nose, and the air seemed to get cleaner with each passing minute. We got to a very narrow part of the cleft, I angled around an edge...and was practically blinded.

"Hang on just a minute, guys, let my eyes get adjusted. There is light coming in, and after being in all of this darkness it is so bright it feels like I am looking directly into the sun."

I lay still for just a moment, allowing my eyes to adjust. I could feel tears streaming down my cheeks, my eyes trying to protect themselves. Then I pulled forward again. The light was about fifteen feet away, up and slightly to the right. Foot by foot, nearer and nearer, and then finally I was at the very edge. I grasped the outer edge with both hands, pulled with all of my might, and popped out into the semi-open sunlight streaming through the boughs of the scraggly firs that were dotting the top of the mountain. Carrie popped out next, then Aly.

We just lay there on our backs, trying to remember what it was like to be able to move freely. Then Aly started to speak, and when she did, a terrifying, "stop your sister, now" kind of thought popped into my head. I immediately reached over and clamped my hand over her mouth.

Both of my sisters knew that I would never do anything like that without a good reason. I put a finger from my other hand up to my lips, made the "shush" sign, and then whispered, "What if that Indian knows about this shaft leading out of the cave?"

Carrie and Aly both went ashen white. Slowly, not making a sound, I rolled over onto my stomach, up onto my knees, and took stock of our surroundings.

We were on the top of a mountain crest, with other crests around us rising a bit higher still. There were large rocks and outcroppings up here, mixed in with a few sparse trees. The hole we had just popped out of was underneath one of those rocks, and truthfully, looked like a large groundhog hole. It was absolutely hidden from view unless one was in this exact spot, looking down at just the right angle. It is very likely that we were the only human beings that even knew about it. Very likely, but not at all one hundred percent certain.

Judging pretty well which direction we had come from while running and then climbing, I belly crawled toward the western side of this plateau. I slowly looked over, remembering that in the woods, it is almost always movement that catches the eye.

And then I had to catch myself to keep from laughing. For there, a good way below, was the top of a brown skinned head, adorned with a long white feather, sticking out from behind a tree, clearly watching what must be the entrance of the cave we had all run into. He had no idea that we had escaped; he thought we were still trapped and was still waiting for us.

I crawled back over to the girls.

"Good news, Night Heroes, old 'Shoot first and ask questions later' is still guarding the cave entrance. He has no idea we are free. Let's ease down the other side and get long gone before he thinks to look up here, then let's find a place to hole up and go to sleep for our nightly trip home. We'll come back tomorrow better prepared, and hopefully can start the day on offense rather than defense.

And with that we made our way quietly down the other side and found a place a few hundred yards away under the boughs of some low hanging branches to plan, and rest, and sleep, and go home.

Chapter Five

We woke up to the sounds of mom bustling about the hotel room and dad snoring softly. Carrie looked over the edge of the bed to where I was laying on my sleeping bag on the floor.

"Some way to begin an adventure, huh, big brother?" she whispered.

"Yeah, I would surely say so. I think we need to file a grievance with the Union of Night Heroes," I said with a grin.

Aly peeked her head over the edge of the bed too at that point.

"How exactly are we going to manage this one?" she asked. "Normally we have the option of researching the area, getting our bearings, and figuring out from our studies in this time what we are supposed to be doing in the past. Somehow I doubt that there's much research that can be done in the 21st century to tell us what to do in the mountain passes of the 18th century in Tennessee during a blood feud between the Indians and the white man!"

"No," I said, "you're probably right on that. I think we will have to do this one a lot more on-the-fly than normal."

And then came that gruff voice that somehow always made me jump out of my skin every time I first heard it in the morning.

"If you guys are going to be laying there whispering and giggling, you need to get your lazy selves on out of bed and get up and get ready for the day."

When dad spoke, it never really was a suggestion even if it was a suggestion. He is a firm believer in the biblical model; when the head of the home speaks, the children in the home do as they are told. Not that any of us minded. Our home is a happy, joyful, laughing, wonderful place to grow up. My dad knows how to be a dad, my mom knows how to be a mom, and all of us enjoy our family thoroughly.

With no hesitation at all we were up and about our morning routine. The girls primped and sprayed and puffed and powdered. Dad shaved, and I looked in the mirror really carefully to see if I needed to shave yet.

"Not quite yet, Twinkie," dad said with a grin, "not quite yet."

All things considered it didn't take us long to be ready to get out the door. Dad is hyper if nothing else, and when he gets rolling in the morning, he wants to get moving quickly. It is as if he treasures each and every moment of each and every day, and wants to squeeze every drop out of life that he possibly can. I guess that's because he knows that every day really is a gift from God and one doesn't know when any particular day may be his last. That being the case, a person should live every day of his life to please the Lord, and to enjoy the life that God has given him.

Once we were up and about, we went down to the hotel lobby and had a delicious continental breakfast. From there it was down to Rogersville, where I knew that we would be looking around at whatever historical sites that there were to see.

One of the first things that we managed to find was, of all things, an old cemetery. It may sound kind of odd to look for something like that, but the Rogersville Cemetery has graves that date way back into the early 1700s. Markers like that certainly tell a story, each and every one of them.

Suddenly I heard Carrie beside me suck in her breath and gasp. I turned to see what it was that caught her attention and suddenly found myself gasping as well.

"Wow," Carrie said while shaking her head, "here it is, the actual grave site of the grandparents of Davy Crockett. Proof written in stone of just how bad the bloodshed really is, or rather was, between the Indians and the white man."

"Right, Sis, and this is the trouble that little Samuel is swept up in."

"Let's hope we can get to him before it is too late," Aly said grimly, "I would hate to think of a little grave marker somewhere with his name on it too."

Once we were done at the cemetery mom and dad took us back into town. It was about time for lunch, and little did we know that we were about to get a very rare treat. We ended up at a little place called the Hale Inn, or the Hale Spring Hotel. It has been in existence and continuous operation since 1824.

For the record, that was one of the best meals, ever. I had the pork chop lunch. The chops were absolutely amazing beyond description, rivaled only by the Bell Buckle Café, if at all. They were cooked in a creamy garlic sauce and were as tender as the finest steak. The corn was so naturally sweet that it needed no salt at all. The ranch dressing was homemade and was good and strong.

We came back to the hotel for a bit, then went back to the Hale Inn for a tour once their lunch hour was over. We learned that the hard wood floor was original, dating back to 1824. It has been walked on by three presidents: Andrew Jackson, Andrew Johnson, and James

Polk. The rooms are really amazing, and dad said that he and mom may try to come back and stay there some day.

From there we went back to the hotel, dad got in some prayer and study time, and then we met the pastor for supper at El Paraiso Mexican restaurant. It was very good. After that we went to the church. Service went very well, my dad preached a message called "The Difference between Conformities and Convictions." That is a really soul-searching kind of a message. A lot of times we do what we do simply because it is what is expected of us, rather than because it is what we know is right. But if that is the case, then when no one is around or no one is making us do right, we probably will stop doing right. I hope I never do that. I really want to live for the Lord my whole life even if no one else does.

After church we got back to the hotel, went through our nightly routine, prayed, hugged, said our good nights, and bedded down for what, I was quite sure, was going to be another very eventful night of "rest."

Chapter Six

Somewhere in the middle of my dreams it began to feel a little bit as if the bed was rocking from side to side. Like dad, I tend to get motion sick, so it didn't take me long to wake up once I felt that rocking sensation.

As soon as my eyes opened, they were greeted by the bright sunlight filtering through the boughs of trees on either side of the river.

"Good morning, Kyle. I am pleased to announce that the second day of the adventure is apparently starting much more peacefully than the first," the Conductor said with a smile as I looked up at him.

I sat up and looked around me and saw that I was in a canoe. The Conductor was in the back of the canoe with a paddle in his hands and a smile on his face, I was in the middle of the canoe, and Carrie and Aly were up front.

"Has it ever occurred to you, Kyle, that you are always the last one of us to wake up?" Aly said with a bit of a smug tone of voice.

"Hey, I'm the one that has to do most of the heavy lifting okay?"

"Ohhh, riggghhht," she said. "I had forgotten that, Mr. Wannabe Hercules."

"Pipe down, squirt, and let's get started. Good morning, Mr. Conductor, and somehow I'm not surprised to see you mastering yet another form of transportation!"

"Thank you, young man, and good morning to you as well. I trust all three of you are ready to begin day two of your adventure?"

"Absolutely," we all answered at once.

"Excellent," he said, "because, as always, time is of the essence. Yesterday you met your antagonist, Black Crow. Obviously you did not meet him face-to-face, but rather were the recipients of his rather pointed messages."

Now that was a surprise, I thought to myself with a giggle, our Conductor himself is not above humor and puns!

"Yes, sir, we certainly did and were, but I suppose today we are going to have to be a little more proactive, rather than running for our lives. Yesterday we were in the trees, but I see that today we are beginning out on the river."

"That is correct," he said. "Carrie, do you have any idea where we are?"

"Well sir, I would say that this is most likely the Holston River. If it is, then we could be within two or three miles of Rogersville. We could also be several hundred miles away, as the Holston extends way down into Cherokee territory."

"Correct on all counts," he said. "And you are, in fact, at this point about twenty miles outside of Rogersville. If all goes well I should be able to put you three ashore just outside of Creek territory. From there it will be up to you to scout out the terrain and to see what you can do about rescuing little Samuel."

That was all very simple and straightforward, so for a little while we simply rode downstream in silence, the only noises being the paddle breaking the water gently and the birds in the trees on either side of the river. Such a peaceful, idyllic scene, but that peace was clearly only illusory. Under the surface there was hatred and violence, and a very precious life on the line.

After a little while I shook the mental cobwebs out of my head, and said, "Hey, guys, before we go ashore let's start the second day of our adventure the way we ought to start every day." And without any further explanation four heads immediately bowed, eight eyes immediately closed, and every heart present in that boat began to make intercession before the throne of God.

After a few minutes there were the sounds of several murmured "amens." Sometimes we pray out loud, but sometimes we simply pray silently, knowing that the Lord is capable of hearing either way.

In maybe another ten minutes or so, we rounded a bend in the river and saw a sandbar three or four hundred yards ahead. The Conductor made straight for it, and in just a couple of minutes the canoe slid up on to the bank.

"This is where you three get off," the Conductor said, "and may you have Godspeed on this day."

We all stepped out of the boat, took our little packs that we had gone to bed with the night before that contained things that we all thought may be helpful somehow, and the Conductor slid the canoe back out into the river. Within a few moments he was gone, and we were on our own in the wilderness of Tennessee.

Chapter Seven

"Well, here we are. What's first?" Aly asked.

It was good to hear her ask that question. Normally she would just have run into the woods looking for someone to pounce on. Maybe she was getting a little bit more careful.

"Well, I'm thinking that the first thing we need to do is get our directional bearings. It's early morning, the sun is coming up to our left as we face down river, so I would say that the river is going south, to our left is east, the way we came from is north, and across the river is west.

"Based on where we were yesterday, then, I would say that we are on the correct side of the river and that we need to work our way inland and back to the north just a bit. What do you think, Carrie, does that sound about right?"

"Yep, I would say so."

"Excellent. Then let's get started. Before we do, some things to keep in mind. Number one, we need to be very quiet as we go. Any Indians near us are likely to have better trained ears than we do. Any small noise to us will probably sound like a freight train coming through to them. Watch where you put your feet. Be careful not to step on any twigs in the pathway, as the noise of them breaking will be huge.

"Secondly, unless we come under attack, make all of your movements slow and smooth. Any quick movements will be able to be seen from a long way away. The main things we need to accomplish today are to try to find where the Creek Indians have made their camp to see if we can scout it out to find Samuel and to find a way to get him out. Ideally we can find all of them and all of that without any of them finding us first."

We started off into the trees, being as careful, quiet, and smooth as 21st century kids could possibly be in the wilderness of the 18th century. As we went, we couldn't help but be amazed at the size of the trees. The old-growth timber simply dwarfed most of the trees in our modern world.

Moving through the trees was definitely nothing new to us, not since our adventure in Germany of World War II. What definitely was new was realizing that the enemy we now faced was not an enemy who marched in ranks and made noise as he went, but an enemy who could blend in with the trees and the surroundings so successfully as to be able to bring death before one even knew that death was upon him.

We really had no way of knowing if we were making our way the right direction exactly. We just knew a general area that we needed to be searching.

For a good while we simply made our way through the trees wandering a bit aimlessly. I was out front with Aly behind me and Carrie behind her. It all seemed very much identical: tree after tree after tree, bird, squirrel bird, squirrel, rock, tree. If this was all that we saw, we were going to have a very hard time rescuing anybody!

I was musing on all of that "sameness," when from somewhere a part of a Bible verse made its way into my mind, "a wise man's heart discerneth both time and judgment."

"What?" Carrie said quietly in response to my mumbling.

"Ecclesiastes 8:5. It basically means that a wise person pays very close attention to things." Then I grinned and said, "Things like those deer tracks ahead of us. I've been spending so much time looking around at the trees that all look the same, and the rocks that all look the same, that I haven't been paying attention to the ground. There is an almost imperceptible trail where deer have been walking through the years."

"What good does that do us?" Aly asked, "We aren't looking for deer; we're looking for Indians!"

"It does us a lot of good, actually, because a person is very unlikely to ever see Indian tracks. They wore soft moccasins and tended not to leave tracks. But they almost always walked the same pathways that the animals walked. Find an animal trail and you have very likely found an Indian trail too. Let's follow this small pathway and see where it leads."

The tracks led away to the right and up the hill. It was a very, very narrow trail, and sometimes it was hard to find, but somehow we always managed to pick it back up. After about an hour it weaved back around to the left a bit, in between some large rocks, and to the very edge of a rock outcropping overlooking a cliff of about one hundred feet high. We made our way to the edge of the cliff, looked around and were at a complete loss as to what to do from there.

"What do we do now, jump?" Aly said.

"No, definitely not. The first thing we do is pay attention, very close attention, to that thin little trail of smoke down in the valley away to our right. That, I would say, is the direction that we need to be heading. The second thing we do is find out how the deer got off of this cliff. I guarantee you they didn't jump, so there has to be a way down that we don't see yet."

We split up on top of that plateau and began to look around. It didn't take long for Carrie to whistle for Aly and I to head her direction. When we got to her we saw it, a narrow opening between the rocks so well hidden behind a bush that you would never see it unless standing right on it. The bush was a bit brushed to one side, and had little brown patches of fur lodged in its branches.

"Good catch, Sis, this is definitely the way down. Everybody fall in line, and let's make our way very carefully this direction. Remember that a deer has better traction than you do, so we're gonna need to go slow."

Very meticulously and carefully we made our way down through the rocks. It was a winding pathway sometimes no wider than a foot. There were a lot of pretty scary places where there was very little to grab onto and a very long way to fall. It is moments like that that will make you very glad that you are saved and know that you are on your way to heaven. Even so, I wasn't exactly anxious to go right then, so I was very careful with every step. I looked back periodically and saw that Carrie and Aly were being just as careful as I was.

It took us maybe an hour to get to the bottom. When we did, we looked up where we had come from and shook our heads in amazement. That is definitely not something that we wanted to do every single day.

"Okay, guys, now we make our way off to the right a bit and forward. That smoke couldn't have been more than a couple of miles away, so walk carefully and be quiet."

The trail was a little more visible down here in the bottom. One reason for that, I suppose, is that a little creek ran right beside it. This no doubt emptied out into the Holston River at some point, but for now was serving as a handy-dandy guide for us to walk beside. Indians were no different than anybody else– they needed water to live. I guessed that there was an above average probability that their camp, where the smoke was coming up from, was probably right beside the creek.

We moved as stealthily as possible, while still trying to maintain a reasonable pace. We didn't know what we would find when or if we got there, so we wanted some time to spare. We could normally cover two miles in a very short period of time. On a dead run, there's none of us that would've taken more than twenty minutes to do it. But going as carefully as we were, I judged that it would take us probably three or four hours to cover the distance.

The first hour and a half was very uneventful, and despite the fact that we knew we were getting closer to the camp, it was actually a very peaceful walk. Peaceful enough, in fact, to lull me into a "non-discerning" state. And that carelessness nearly cost me my life.

Chapter Eight

For a good while I had been watching the trail carefully as we went. But lulled by the sameness of it all once again, at some point I had started looking up into the trees as we went. For whatever reason, I guess probably just the goodness of God, I looked down before I took my next step. Had I not done so, this story would've turned out very different. There, in the path right ahead of me, right where I was about to step, was a rattlesnake.

I froze.

Carrie behind me saw me stop with one foot in the air, and bless her heart and quick thinking she immediately stopped as well and put a hand out to stop Aly, too. If she had not done so, she would have knocked me right into that snake, who was already clearly very angry at us three interlopers into his territory.

I am telling you, that snake was massive. I recognized it immediately as a timber rattler, the most lethal of snakes in the area, one of the most lethal in the world, in fact. His body was as big around as a baseball bat, and easily four or five feet long. His tail was now twitching like a house afire, and to me was producing a deafeningly loud sound. The look on his face was pure evil and malice, as if he was savoring every moment of this and was really going to enjoy what came next.

I knew that if he got me, I was as good as dead.

Behind me I could hear Aly begin to whimper. Carrie was not making a sound. I was still standing on one leg, with the leg that I had been intending to put down as my next step still hanging there in the air. I knew I couldn't stay that way very long, but I also knew that I could not take that next step.

"Kyle," Carrie whispered very quietly and calmly, "this appears to be a problem."

"Uh, yeah," I whispered back, "I would say so. Do you have any brilliant ideas, before this snake decides to take me out?"

"Well, you're clearly too close to it to be able to move away from it quick enough. If you move at all, he is going to strike, and he won't miss at that distance. But if we wait much longer, he is going to strike anyway, he is getting more agitated by the second."

"Do you have any good news, Socrates?" Beads of sweat were starting to pop out on my forehead, and my one grounded leg was beginning to shake and wobble.

"Be calm, give me some time to think," she said.

"Time to think?" I said with growing agitation of my own. "Time seems to be the one thing I don't have much of, Sis, so can we please-"

It was a blur from there, with things happening so quickly that they at once seemed to be both lightning fast and happening in slow motion. I heard a snapping sound from behind me, I saw the snake strike, and then I saw it writhing on the ground just in front of me as if it was in the throes of death. Without even thinking, I dove backward onto the ground, and rolled up on to one knee. Aly was standing right beside me with her left arm out in front of her, and her right arm drawn back. Her slingshot was held firmly in her outstretched left hand.

That explained the snapping sound behind me.

"Seriously, little sister? Don't you think you should warn me before you take a risk like that with my life on the line?"

"You two seemed to be having such a peaceful philosophical discussion, I felt like it would be rude to bother you. Besides, I needed to focus on what I was doing so I could get close with my shot."

"Close! Close?!? You mean you weren't actually trying to hit it?" I said incredulously.

"Of course I was trying to hit it, Kyle, but with a target as small as a snake's head, even somebody as good as me with a slingshot might not be able to do that. But I didn't have to. I knew that if I got close enough the snake would do the rest of the work for me by striking at the whizzing rock. And please, no thank yous, just throw money..."

"Cute, Sis, real cute. But believe me, you'd be worth every penny of every dollar I could throw. You just saved my life; I owe you one."

"Let's hope you never have to pay up on that one," she said with a huge grin.

"I hear that," I said with a grin of my own. "And now, let's take what may prove to be a handy little trophy." With that, I pulled a pocket knife out of my pack, waited a few more minutes for the snake to completely stop wriggling so I could be sure it was dead, and then I cut off its rattles.

"What you have in mind with that?"

"This, my big-brained sister, could very well be helpful in our dealings with the Indians. Anyone who can kill a snake like this will have some credibility. I have no idea how or if this may come into play, but it certainly won't hurt to have it."

After an exciting episode like that, we figured it would be a good time to take a few minutes' worth of a break. We went back into the trees just a bit, and sat down beside the deadfall of an old log. We took a minute to thank the Lord for sparing my life, and then we did something we had never thought of doing.

"Hey, guys," I said, "do you realize that right now while we're awake in 1778, Mom and Dad are asleep in our time? All of us know that they spend a lot of time while we're asleep at night praying for us. Why don't we take a few minutes now while we know that they're asleep and pray for them?"

"Now that is a cool thought," Carrie said with a surprised look on her face. "I had never thought of that."

And so we prayed for the two people that we love most in life, the two people who would surely worry themselves sick if they knew what we were doing right now.

Chapter Nine

Once we finished praying we knew that it was time to get back about our business. We got back to the trail and started working our way toward where we assumed that the Creek Indian camp would be. For myself, I was for some reason watching the trail much more carefully than I had been before.

After about another hour and a half, I pulled up to a dead stop, but this time not because of a snake in the pathway. We had come to the edge of the little hill and the smell of smoke from the valley down below it was pretty strong. Without having to say a word, all three of us did as we had learned to do. We got down on our bellies and crawled toward the edge of the hill.

When we looked over the edge, I couldn't help but grin. There below us in a relatively open spot in the trees was the beautifully organized camp of the Creek Indians. In the very center there was a prominent teepee made of alternating coverings of black and brown. It had spears stuck in the ground outside of the opening, and each one of the spears had a lovely headdress hanging on it. This had to be the teepee of the chief himself. Around it, spread out from the center in such perfect organization that it looked like it had been laid out by an architect, were at least thirty more teepees a bit smaller and less elaborate than the first.

On the outside of the camp in four corners were horses picketed in the grass. The creek made a bend right past the camp, a ninety-degree turn, and went off to the west. The spot they had chosen for camp was absolutely ideal. It was well watered, plenty of grass for the horses, and had a decent field of vision in all directions. No one could approach that camp without being seen.

Across the creek weaving back to the northeast there was a clear pathway leading up into the hills, a good way of escape should anyone attack from our side. It dawned on me that the path that we were now on would also make an excellent way of escape should anyone attack from the other side. They really had thought of everything: provision, defense, and escape. The chief of this tribe may be many things, but he was clearly no dummy.

In all of the organization, there was one thing that stuck out as being out of place. There was a square enclosure toward the edge of the camp near to where one section of the horses were picketed. It was made all of wood and had a bar across the opening both on the top and the bottom, keeping the door firmly fastened shut from the outside.

"That's it, guys, that's where they'll be holding Samuel."

We lay there for a few minutes examining the situation very carefully. There really was no good way to get into that camp or near to that makeshift prison without being seen.

"We're sort of at a dead end here, aren't we?" asked Carrie.

"It sure looks like it, Sis, it sure looks like it, at least for the time being."

"Then if we're at a dead end for now," Aly said impatiently, "why don't we go back into the trees and find something else to do until time to go to sleep for our nightly ride home? I sure don't want to stay here looking at nothing happening for the indefinite future."

"Be patient, Sis, you're getting more and more like your grandfather every day."

She really was. Our grandfather, God bless him, is about the most impatient man alive. Not in a bad sort of way, he just can't stand to sit still for even a moment. Come to think of it, dad is a lot like that too. No wonder we kids tend to be the same way.

We sat there watching for a good while even though all of us were anxious to be doing something. There really was nothing we could do at the moment, but I've learned in my short fourteen years that when people are patient enough to wait and to watch, often some very good things will happen. And praise the Lord that surely proved to be true in this instance.

Carrie saw it first.

"Look!" She hissed.

I let my gaze follow the direction of her outstretched finger and saw what she was so intently pointing at. Coming toward the camp from straight ahead of us on the other side of the creek was one lone covered wagon. It was being driven by an unusual looking character in buckskins, with a long white beard, and a raccoon hat. He appeared to be a white man, and yet the Indians seemed not to be the least bit alarmed at his presence.

"Trader," I said. A man with good solid tools and weapons, willing to sell them to the Indians, would be welcomed in their presence without any question.

We watched as the trader crossed the creek, his wagon pulled by a sturdy looking mule. He pulled up into the edge of the camp, and it seemed that from every teepee Indians issued forth immediately.

"It's an ancient ice cream truck!" Aly giggled.

"That's funny, Sis," I said, "I can almost hear the calliope music playing from the back."

We watched as the trader pulled his wagon to a stop, got down from his perch, and bowed to greet the Indians who were coming to him. They all seemed to be on very friendly terms, and there was a great deal of jockeying for position as he rolled back the covering from the wagon and began to show the wares and supplies that he had available on that day.

The buying and trading went on at a brisk pace, until suddenly everything changed and it all stopped. The crowd of Indians in front of the wagon parted as if it had been the Red Sea under the staff of Moses. All of the Indians bowed low, as did the trader himself. There, walking to their midst, was an old man, and two boys, one either side of him.

"That has to be the chief and Black Crow and Falling Rain," I said.

"How will we know which one is which?" Aly asked.

"That shouldn't be too hard, I don't think. From what the Conductor said we should be able to tell by their attitudes which of the two boys is which."

Boy, was I ever right about that one.

The chief politely returned the bow of the trader, then stuck out his right arm and clasped the outstretched right arm of the white man who'd come into their midst. The young man on the right of the chief then did the exact same thing. But when the trader turned to the young man on the chief's left, there was no bow nor was there any outstretched hand, there was simply a question that was really more of a demand. "Do you have them?"

It was remarkably good English and very forcefully spoken.

The trader quickly answered, "Yes, great warrior, I have at least the one you most desire."

The trader turned back to his wagon, and I saw him reach deep inside a wooden box. He pulled back out an object wrapped in what looked to be an expensive leather cloth. I watched as he unwrapped the item, laid the cloth aside and then extended his hands toward Black Crow. The way the sun glinted off of the item in his hands, there was no doubt in my mind what it was.

"Just as the great warrior has required," the trader said, "made of the finest steel, and never will you find one sharper."

Black Crow held that knife up to the sun, and it was as polished as a mirror. It had to be fully twelve inches long, and the way his hand wrapped around the handle, it seemed to be very sturdily made.

"An excellent weapon," Black Crow said with a sneer, "fit for killing man or beast, or for a man who is a beast."

As soon as the last word came out of his mouth, Black Crow whirled around as fast as lightning, letting out a yell as he spun, and threw that knife harder than a major league baseball pitcher could ever dream of throwing a baseball. It cut through the air like the hammer of Thor and slammed into the side of the wooden enclosure that Samuel was being held captive in.

It sunk in all the way to the handle, as if it had been thrown into hot butter.

Black Crow turned back to the trader, pulled what I assumed to be a couple of pieces of gold or silver out of the pouch that he had on his side, dropped them into the trader's hand, and without so much as a thank you turned and walked away from him.

"See that you are here with the rest before the festival tomorrow night," he said without turning around."

"As you wish, Black Crow."

"I think we've seen all we need to see for the day, guys. While Black Crow is retrieving his new toy, let's slide back up into the trees and get ready to go home for the night. Very clearly, we have our work cut out for us."

Chapter Ten

It was a blessing to wake up in room 203 of the Comfort Inn once again.

"What do you think, Kyle?" Aly said as she leaned over the bed.

"I think that kid is nothing to be taken lightly," I said. "He's almost as big as I am, pretty strong I would say judging from how far he threw that knife, and that knife itself looks like you could do surgery with it."

"One thing we do know," Carrie said, "is that there's no way Samuel can handle anybody like that. If we don't get him out of there, he is absolutely done for."

"Agreed. But I may know how we can do it. Black Crow told the trader that there's going to be a festival tomorrow night. Let's hope the old movies about cowboys and Indians weren't too far off base, and that the festival is going to include a bonfire, dancing, and a whole lot of whooping and hollering. If it does, that should provide us all the distraction that we need to get little Samuel out of there."

Not much more needed to be said on that, so we began the morning routine of once again primping and poofing and powdering and brushing. Before we knew it, we were out the door and heading out in search of fun and adventure again. Not adventure like we kids are used to, but at least what my dad would consider adventure.

We headed out of Rogersville, maybe forty-five minutes or so, and eventually pulled up at a place that apparently my dad knew about called Gray's Fossil Site. If anything has anything to do with fossils or rocks and minerals, I can guarantee you my dad is interested.

We went inside and looked around; it is a museum owned and operated by East Tennessee State University. The fossils themselves were really cool, but sadly, as is to be expected I suppose, the entire place was overtly evolutionistic. Fortunately we kids have learned to see through foolishness like that. My dad has a sharp enough brain to think through things logically, and he's taught us to do the same thing.

Just the fact that the Bible tells us "In the beginning God created the heaven and earth," should be enough. But the fact of the matter is we have far more to go on than just that. Real science supports the Bible, and destroys the idea of evolution. Did you know, for instance, that there has never been a single "missing link" ever found? There are pictures of them in every textbook, but the artists may as well be drawing pictures of *Alice's Adventures in Wonderland*, because they are both made up. Dinosaurs are supposed to have lived 250 million years ago, missing links are supposed to have lived between one and three million years ago, yet there are tens of thousands of intact dinosaur fossils and skeletons but not one missing link skeleton.

Through the years people have found a tooth here, a fragment of the skull there, and then used Plaster of Paris and imagination to produce their "missing links." All of the bone fragments that make up all of the so-called missing links could be put into a very small box. If missing links were so very recent and dinosaurs were so very ancient, the exact opposite should be true. We should be finding very few dinosaur skeletons and tens of thousands of missing link skeletons. The reason we aren't finding any missing link skeletons, is because the missing link is still missing. And the reason the missing link is still missing is because there never was a missing link! In the beginning God created the heaven and the earth.

Anyway, despite all of the ridiculous evolution stuff, the fossils themselves really were very cool. 250 million years old? Nah, more like five or six thousand years old, but still very cool.

Once we finished up there, we ran back toward Rogersville, did some shopping, grabbed some lunch at a local pizza joint, and headed back to the hotel. Dad spent the rest of the afternoon studying and preparing for the service; the rest of us did our school work. That is one of the drawbacks of being evangelist's kids; everywhere you go is school, and you still have to do the same amount of days and the same amount of work as anybody in a traditional school.

The evening came soon enough, we got dressed, ran out and grabbed a quick bite of supper, and headed on to the church. The service that night went really well. Dad preached a message about Noah's ark called "Still Alive but Already Dead." A fifteen-year-old young man got saved, and there was plenty of weeping and rejoicing around the altar.

After church we went out and fellowshipped with the pastor and his family for a little while in the fellowship hall. Then it was back to the hotel for another night of rest for my parents and action for us Night Heroes.

Chapter Eleven

Once again it was the gentle rocking of the canoe and the lapping of the waves against the side of it that awakened all three of us. There at the back of the boat, in his place as always, was our Conductor. His paddle broke the water in rythmatic fashion, making nary a sound as he propelled us through the brownish water.

"Good evening, Night Heroes, and good morning as well."

Carrie, perpetually cheerful, grinned up at him. "Good me-ve-ning to you as well, sir!"

"I trust you are ready for your third day in action," he said. "Both Samuel and his invalid father are depending on you."

"We certainly are, sir. My sisters and I think that we have a pretty foolproof plan for getting him out of there, and we brought along a few tools to help us."

I patted my backpack as I said this. Being able to bring things along with us from our time certainly did help to level the playing field just a bit while we were in enemy territory.

"Foolproof plan?" The Conductor asked with only a hint of amusement. "You might have wanted to come up with a 'shrewd and cunning proof' plan, because Black Crow is certainly no fool. Ruthless, cold, calculating, but certainly not an unintelligent simpleton to be taken lightly."

I thought on that for just a while and then asked our Conductor a question. "Tell me, sir, since you clearly know a great deal more about Black Crow than we do, how does he do at controlling his temper? Is he quick to anger?"

A huge smile instantly flashed across the Conductor's face, it was clear he knew what I was thinking.

"As a matter of fact, given the right stimulus, he can be incredibly quick to anger.

It is not his normal habit, but there are areas in which he does have a terribly short fuse."

"I think I know what you're thinking, Bro," Carrie said. "Black Crow may not be a fool, but under the right circumstances we may be able to turn him into one. Ecclesiastes 7:9 says 'Be not hasty in thy spirit to be angry: for anger resteth in the bosom of fools.' Proverbs 25:28 says 'He that hath no rule over his own spirit is like a city that is broken down, and without walls.' If there are buttons that we can push to make Black Crow blow up in a fit of anger, he will become a fool, he will become like a city with no defenses. It's a dangerous game to play, but it's certainly something to keep in mind as an option in case we need it."

We paddled on in silence for a while, and I could not help but be awed at the amazing creation of God all around us. Turtles were bobbing up near the boat without fear, seeming to regard us as oddities to be explored as we passed. Long necked birds, some kind of crane I was guessing, waded at the edge of the river looking for fish to snap up in their beaks as quick as lightning and then swallow down their gullets.

"Look!" Aly hissed.

We all followed her finger as she pointed to the right bank of the river. There near the water's edge was a big black bear and two cubs. That mama bear sniffed and snuffed at the air in our direction, and then stood up on her hind legs as if to get a better look at us. Man, that was one big bear!

"That's one teddy bear I don't think I'd want wrestle with," Carrie said with a whistle and a grin.

"I hear that," I said as I grinned back. "But you know, since we all came from the same pollywog crawling out of the primordial ooze billions and billions of years ago, maybe she just thinks she recognizes us from pictures in the family album."

Carrie, ever the genius and ever logical, rolled her eyes and began to lecture me even though she knew it was not needed.

"And pray tell where did the plant life on earth come from? Did descendants of the pollywog sit still so long that they began to grow roots? And what exactly did the pollywog and its descendants eat in the millions of years that plant life was evolving? How did they not starve to death? And how did either the pollywogs and their descendants and the plants themselves continue to survive in the millions of years that it took for their reproductive systems to form?"

"I get it, Sis, I get it. You can stop lecturing now; even the bear clearly doesn't want to hear it."

The Conductor broke into a big belly laugh at that, for he was the first one other than me to turn and see the mama bear and her cubs running off into the woods.

"Ha ha, very funny. And you," Carrie shouted at the bear and her cubs, "you would be better off hanging out with the fish, since they at least have the sense to appreciate a good day in school!"

All of us laughed at that, and then we settled back into our own thoughts and musings as we continued on down river to the drop-off site.

Finally we arrived at the same spot as yesterday and slid the canoe up onto the bank once again.

"Thank you for the ride, sir," Carrie chimed, and we all added in our agreement with that sentiment.

"You are quite welcome, Night Heroes. Godspeed once again, be careful, and be quick."

And with that he left us, paddling down the stream and fading out of sight around the bend.

"Well, here we go. We know the direction we are traveling this time, so that in itself is an advantage. We also know what our battle plan is. And, since it requires a bit of darkness, we have all day to get there and get set up. So what say we stroll today rather than wasting our energy running?"

Aly wrinkled up her nose at that, clearly not liking the idea. Her boundless energy would need some outlet, or she would give us grief all day long.

"Easy, munchkin, there will be plenty of time for you to go crazy later. In the meantime, we all need to keep our eyes and ears open and go softly and quietly again today. It would be very bad for us to be captured or killed while on the way to rescue someone."

After a quick prayer, we made our way along the same trail as we had the day before. For myself, I carefully watched the pathway ahead of us. My hand went into my pocket from time to time, as I absentmindedly fiddled with the rattles I cut off of the snake the day before. It is sort of weird to think, from time to time, of how near to death we often come.

Everyone seems to think that they will live to a ripe old age, but no one has that guarantee. James 4:14 says, "Whereas ye know not what shall be on the morrow. For what is your life? It is even a vapour, that appeareth for a little time, and then vanisheth away."

All of us knew that, even for a young person, death could come at any moment. That we will all die is certain, but the timing is utterly uncertain. Many a boy figures on growing up, getting married, having kids, and growing old, but never even makes it to the growing up part. That truth makes me glad that I am going to live forever. Not here, no, but I really will live forever! My sisters will too. We all know Jesus as our Savior, so all of us get to live forever in heaven.

"I'm looking forward to it too, Kyle. It really is going to be awesome."

"What?" I said as I snapped back to our present setting.

"Going to heaven," Carrie said. "It is going to be really cool."

"But, how did..."

She just smiled. "You were humming 'What a Day That Will Be.' It doesn't take a brainiac to figure out what was on your mind."

"Sis," I grinned, "you really should consider a career in the FBI when you grow up. You will totally freak some terrorists out by being able to practically read their minds."

She smiled back at me, and we walked on in silence. Sometimes, no words are necessary, especially when God is doing the talking. There was a crisp breeze blowing through the trees, and we could hear the rattle of large oak leaves beating up against each other. Birds were calling to each other, and from somewhere off in the hills I could hear the lone cry of a wolf. Call all of that what you will, I call it God practically shouting, "I did this!"

A few hours later we arrived at the same overlook as yesterday. The camp was utterly unchanged, save for a stringer of fish hanging over a low fire, being smoked and prepared for the festival.

"Okay, guys," I whispered, "here we are. Let's get everything set up for Operation Chicken Run McQueen."

Anyone our age reading this will probably not understand that last reference, so a bit of explanation is in order, I suppose. *Chicken Run* is a cool animated movie that is a takeoff of a movie from 1963 called *The Great*

Escape, starring a guy named Steve McQueen. That movie was based on a true story about a bunch of guys during World War II digging a tunnel and escaping from a POW camp.

We weren't planning on digging a tunnel, but we were planning on a great escape.

We had thoroughly discussed and planned how everything would be done well before we arrived. Dad has a bunch of rules he lives by, and he has taught many of them to us. Rule number four is "Preparation prevents panic." We split up, Carrie and Aly circling the camp to the right, me circling it to the left. We had allotted one hour to do our assigned tasks and make our way back to the point we started from. That would allow us time to do everything slowly and silently, hopefully enough so to not be seen or heard.

Chapter Twelve

It seemed like forever, but both parts of the team actually made it back quicker than the time we had allotted.

"How did you guys do?" I whispered nearly breathlessly.

"Easy peasy, lemon squeezy, Bro," Ally said with a thousand watt grin. "This should be more fun than a juicy steak at a vegetarian convention."

I had to laugh at that one, and I knew it would be a while before I could get that mental picture out of my mind.

"Good. Then let's get in position in the woods directly behind the prison box. We will have approximately one hundred yards to cover from the edge of the woods to the back of it once the fun starts. Hopefully this will all work like a charm."

We slid off to our left and slowly back away and further into the trees. It took us maybe twenty minutes to stealthily get to where we wanted to be, and then we waited.

Little by little nature did as God designed it to do, and the sun sank slowly into the west, telling our side of the earth goodbye until the morrow. Stars begin to slowly make themselves known, and a beautiful white moon soon started to rise.

As if heralded on by some unspoken yet clearly understood command, every teepee swung open almost at the same time, and a bee hive of activity ensued. A huge fire was lit in the center of the camp. Young braves came out to wrestle and play, and precious Indian girls gathered around ancient grandmothers as they prepared for the feast. The trader must have come and gone before we ever arrived, for we saw no sight of him the entire time.

"Are you sure everything is set?" I asked for the umpteenth time.

"Yes, Mother, everything is set."

"Har, har, Carrie, that's really cute. Forgive me for being careful, but a lot is resting on my shoulders here."

"Your shoulders? How about OUR shoulders, mister!"

"Easy, Aly," Carrie chided, "Kyle IS fourteen years old. That means he is old enough for pimples, puppy love, and an overinflated sense of his own importance."

I should have pounded her for that, but now was not the time.

The festival began to grow in intensity to match the growing darkness. Still, we waited just a touch longer. I did not want to tip our hand too quickly, the timing needed to be just right.

A few minutes later I felt like the time was just right.

"Okay, Aly, do your magic."

I tell you, the smile on her face was somewhere between angelic and evil. She reached in her backpack and pulled out a little remote control. In the center of camp all of the braves were dancing around the fire, whooping and hollering in an undulating rhythm. I grabbed a lighter out of my pocket, and flicked it to life. Aly's little remote controlled helicopter had a ten foot piece of clear fishing line attached to it, and on the end of that line was a nice long sparkler. From the moment that I lit it I knew that it would burn for exactly three minutes. I hoped that would be enough.

Our plan was to draw everyone away from camp, hopefully making a lot of confusing noises as they went, while I got Samuel out and into the woods.

I lit the sparkler, and Aly took it from there. With a few skillful and smooth movements of her thumbs, the chopper took flight, and immediately there was, what would doubtless appear to the Indians, a ghostly specter making its way over their camp.

The effect was incredible.

Aly set the height of that chopper just perfect. The sparkler was maybe twenty feet off of the ground, slowly making a straight line over everyone's head. All activity and noise came to a dead stop. And then came the money shot. Aly suddenly dropped that helicopter down low enough that the sparkler was about head high...and right toward the face of Black Crow! He stumbled backward and swatted at it as if it was some demonic mosquito. Anticipating that, Aly jerked it upward and out of reach, and then dive bombed him again. Black Crow cried out half in fear, and then leaped forward and swatted at it yet again. Once again Aly jerked it away from him, and he actually fell on his face trying to get to it. He landed in the dust sputtering, and as he did, the fear in the camp changed to laughter. No one knew what was happening, but seeing the great warrior looking up from the ground with his face covered in dirt was too much. The laughter grew to a fevered pitch, and just as I had hoped, Black Crow's temper took over.

He leaped to his feet and let out a furious scream. That stopped everyone's laughter immediately. Aly kept at it. She bombed him once more, and then turned the helicopter toward the other end of camp and zipped it away as fast as it would go.

Black Crow immediately started off in pursuit, clearly intent on destroying this evil fire fly and regaining his lost respect. With a barked command, everyone in camp was on a dead run after him, as he ran after it–straight toward all of the brush piles in every pathway that had been left for them to trip over, slowing them down.

Instantly I was running too. I dared not risk coming around to the front of the prison box and simply lifting the bars, lest someone had been left behind and we be discovered. I slid in behind it, my handy-dandy pry bar from dad's tool box already out and ready for action. I jammed it in between two boards at the bottom, pushed hard, and the bottom of that board popped loose. Carrie and I grabbed underneath it and yanked, and it came off. Within ten seconds we had done the same to the board beside it, and the opening was large enough to work.

I stuck my head in, and huddled there in the corner looking at us was a frightened little boy, wondering what was happening.

"Samuel, come with me," I said firmly. "You have prayed for help, and help is here."

That was all he needed to hear. Instantly he was on his feet and squeezing through the opening. I grabbed him by one hand, Carrie grabbed him by the other. Aly hustled the helicopter back and shoved everything back into her pack, then all of us took off on a dead run into the woods with our little LED flashlight leading the way.

Chapter Thirteen

We ran hard for about twenty minutes. Our main goal was to get enough distance between us and the camp to be well past any initial search parties they may send out once they realized their prisoner was gone.

When we finally slowed to a walk and caught our breath, we introduced ourselves.

"Samuel, my name is Kyle, this is my sister Carrie, and this is my other sister Aly. Are you okay?"

"I am quite well, thank you," he said through ragged breaths. "How did you come to find me?"

"That is not important. What is important is that we get you back home to your father. Do you know the way?"

"Yes, I do. But it is several hours from here even by day. We should set up camp and then travel the rest of the way tomorrow."

The girls and I looked at each other. We knew that we would have to leave him in just a while, and finish getting him home the next day. But I could tell from the look in both Carrie and Aly's eyes that they knew we needed to get him much farther along before we did.

"We will set up camp, but not quite yet. Let's travel hard for a couple more hours before we do, just to get in a safer location."

Samuel and I took the lead, and naturally, the first thing he asked about was my strange "light giving stick." I had to be careful here, and I knew it.

"This is something from the big city" (that was true, we bought it from a Walmart in Charlotte) "and your area does not have them here yet, but one day it will. Let's just regard it as a gift from God and keep moving."

We went quietly but quickly for a good while. The night time forest was filled with sounds: crickets, loons, owls, and the occasional unidentified growl or howl that made the hair on the back of our necks stand up. I really didn't like being in unknown territory in the dark, but I knew something that made it better.

Way back in the book of Daniel, fear came in the night. The executioner from the king was making his way through the city preparing to kill all of the wise men. The knock came on Daniel's door, and when he found out what was happening, he did the smartest thing imaginable, he prayed. When the answer that would save their life came to him, Daniel described God as the one who "knoweth what is in the darkness, and the light dwelleth with him."

Our God knows what is in the dark. He sees what we cannot see, He knows what we do not know. And so we would continue on into the darkness. We would put one foot in front of the other, trusting the God who loves us and gave Himself for us. We had a tiny flashlight, but we had something so much better. We had a personal relationship with the God of whom Daniel said "and the light dwelleth with him."

Chapter Fourteen

The pillow, the air mattress, the sheets, man, I love the feel of all of that.

We had left little Samuel at a fairly cozy makeshift camp in the forest, and explained to him that he needed to wait for us, and that we would be back the next day to help him get the rest of the way home. We went a few hundred yards off into the forest, settled in for our nightly trip home, and now I was stretching and yawning as the morning rays of light began to penetrate the curtains of our comfy hotel room.

"Up and at 'em, Warner Brats, daylight's burning! Move it, move it, move it, move it!"

That would be my dad, "Mr. Morning Peacefulness."

It didn't take long with that kind of motivation for us to be vertical and vivacious. We brushed and rinsed and dressed and combed and sprayed and tidied and straightened. That last part applied to the room, not to us. And why, pray tell, would we straighten a hotel room, when there is maid service each day? That would be my mom, "Mrs. I'm–Not–Going–To–Have–Anyone–Come–And–Clean–In–Here–Till–We–Have–Cleaned–First." Logical? Um, no. Momical? Yes, oh yes.

Once we were ready and the room had been straightened, organized, and sanitized to such a degree that one could eat off of the carpet, we were up and about our day. We loaded up in the Yukon and headed out of town, going toward Abingdon, Virginia. That is about an hour away, and it is where another good friend of my Dad's pastors, a man named Bryan Treadway. Before we knew it we were passing the airport and looking way up on the hill to the left where the beautiful Emmanuel Baptist Church sits. We pulled into the driveway, wound our way up the twisty hill, and went to the parsonage behind the church.

The Treadways are a cool family. That have, like, a million kids or so, all of them as nice as can be. I am good friends with their oldest son, Jonathan. We all hugged and slapped backs and shook hands, then spent a good bit of time in the living room catching up with what had been going on in everyone's life.

At lunchtime we went down to the Cheddars. In case you do not know, that is a place worth going. The food is awesome, especially the chips and queso. Mom and dad always get steaks. The prices are reasonable, too.

We ate and laughed and fellowshipped, then, sadly, it was time to say goodbye for now.

They stood in the parking lot and waved as we drove away. As we left, I mused a bit on the fact that I was friends not just with the kids, but with the adults as well. I looked up to Pastor Treadway, but I still regarded him as a friend, too. Most people may consider that odd, but it is how my father has taught me to be. He loves to quote this verse:

Proverbs 27:10 Thine own friend, and thy father's friend, forsake not; neither go into thy brother's house in the day of thy calamity: for better is a neighbor that is near than a brother far off.

"Son," he will say in his 'dad voice,' "These grown men that I am friends with, make them your friends, too. Older friends are generally wiser friends, and if you are going to grow up right, you are going to need all of the wise friends you can get.

Smart, that.

We made our way back to Rogersville, stopping along the way at a couple of flea markets, a road side boiled-peanut stand, (for mom. Dad says, "If I wanted to eat something that has the texture and taste of a bean, I would eat a bean") and a used book store. Funny how my folks take such pleasure in stuff like that. I guess when you grew up in the age of black and white television, phones hooked to the wall by squiggly cords, and manual typewriters, it doesn't take much to make a person happy.

Once we got back to the hotel, we set into our schoolwork for the day, while dad studied to be ready to preach once service time rolled around. Yes, we are home schooled. No we do not have a football team or a band, but on the bright side, I am at the top of my class every single year, and I do not get suspended for coming to school with a chicken nugget that is vaguely shaped like a gun.

A couple of hours before service we met Pastor Rackley and Mrs. Elisha his wife at Wendy's. We enjoyed the food and the fellowship, but inside of my heart I could feel a stirring, a longing for the adventure to come. Not the one that would come after we went to sleep, but the one we would have at church. What better adventure is there than worshipping the living God and seeing the eternal work He does in hearts?

We were not disappointed. Dad did not even get a chance to preach. During the song service, people started to weep and to testify of how good God has been to them. When that happens, it is usually best just to stand back and see what God does.

An hour and a half later, the altar was wet with grateful tears, a couple of young people had been saved, and we knew that it had nothing to do with any of us Warners. The people of a church had prayed and sought after God, and He had responded. It may not be good grammar, but the best thing I can think of to say is, "Ain't God good!"

Chapter Fifteen

As I lay on my back on my mattress staring up at a ceiling I could not see, my heart was happy and grateful. God had met with us during the service, and lives had been forever changed. The only problem about that kind of happiness is that it can keep a person awake, and I needed to go to sleep.

And then a thought hit me that I had never really thought of before. Some nights I actually cannot go to sleep because my mind just would not stop thinking. If that happened, what would happen to that night's mission? Would all three of us still get to go, or none of us, or only the ones that were asleep? Would this be like a Santa Clause (which none of us ever believed in. No way was dad going to give an obese elf credit for what he bought for us) thing where "He sees you when you're sleeping, he knows when you're awake?"

I had to go to sleep, I could not take the chance on not being there to complete the mission. But you probably know just how hopeless that is. What I mean is, when you try to think of not thinking, you are thinking! Grrrrr!

I counted sheep. I tried breathing really slowly. I tried to think of darkness. Nothing worked. The other four bodies in the room were all snoring gently, sound asleep. I had to join them; I had to go to sleep!

But nothing worked. Try as I might, I was wide awake and could not even begin to sleep. Frustrated and a bit worried, I sat up and looked over at Carrie and Aly up on their bed. But when I did, the strangest thing happened; they slowly looked over at me and with dreamy eyes said, "Goodbye, Kyle, we will miss you..." and then they faded away! Panic set in. I jumped up and looked over at Mom and Dad's bed, and they had that same dreamy look on their faces.

"Goodbye, Kyle, we will miss you too. Don't forget to feed the fish," and then they faded away as well.

Now I was utterly frantic. Everyone was gone! And I didn't know what to feed the fish! Come to think of it, I didn't even know where I had put the fish! And then I remembered, I had put him in my tube of toothpaste. I rushed to the bathroom, grabbed the toothpaste, and squeezed it very hard from the bottom like mom always wants us to do. But when I did, it wasn't just one fish that came out, there were literally hundreds of them, wriggling and squiggling all over and around my feet, and...

"Kyle! Kyle! Dude, wake up, we have work to do!"

It was Aly. I sat straight up in the canoe with a loud gasp.

"Bro," she said, "are you okay? You look like you tossed and turned all night. And who in the world is Nemo?"

I just laughed and shook my head, calmed my racing heart and said, "It doesn't matter. But if dad wants to go out and eat fish tomorrow, tell him I'll have a burger instead."

Even the Conductor looked at me like I had lost my mind.

We paddled on downstream for a while and softly discussed our task for the day. It was pretty simple, really, we needed to meet back up with Samuel and get him the rest of the way home safely.

On this particular day, though, we had him drop us off a mile or so further upstream. Another rule of my dad's is "Patterns prevent problems. Unless you are being followed, in which case patterns cause problems."

I am pretty sure he got that from a Louis L'Amour book, and it makes good sense. As skilled as the Creek Indians were at tracking, the last thing we needed to do was to become predictable.

Once we were ashore, we made our way through the trees in the direction we needed to go. I estimated that it would take us about four or five hours to get there, as long as we did not encounter any difficulty along the way. The day was cool, the beginning of a fall breeze was blowing, and the air was so clean you could almost drink it. From time to time we saw tracks, big ones, that I was quite certain belonged to a very large cat, most likely a mountain lion of 150 pounds or better. That was one critter I definitely did not want to meet up close.

Using both our compass and visible mountain peaks, we pretty easily picked up the trail that we needed to be on. Then we picked up the pace just a little bit, anxious to get back to where we knew Samuel would be waiting for us. Presently, we saw the little knoll over which we knew we would find the campsite. Just to be cautious, we once again got down and belly crawled to where we knew we could see the site without anyone from down there seeing us.

"All seems absolutely quiet down there," Aly said.

"Yeah," Carrie chimed in, "a little too quiet if you ask me. I don't hear anything, and I don't see any movement either."

Well, there wasn't much we could do other than check, so we very carefully eased our way down into the little campsite. It was just as I feared; Samuel was nowhere around.

"Those Indians came and snatched our rescuee," Aly said with a pout. But I wasn't so sure.

"I don't think so, Sis," I said. "Even with all the bare dirt spots in this camp, ground that would absolutely show signs of any type of struggle, there's nothing. Not a moccasin print, not a horse hoof, not a broken branch, no evidence that Indians have been here at all. Everybody be very still and let me just look around for a minute."

I tried to remember everything I had ever read and everything my dad had ever told me about tracking. He and I had spent a lot of time out in the woods together hiking and watching and noticing. The forest is a lot like a book, if you can just decipher the language.

Pretty soon, I thought I had a reasonably good idea of what had happened.

"Check this out, guys. See these little indentations in the dirt? Every one of them is the same distance apart, about the distance of a boy's step. These have to be Samuel's. The fact that there is nothing else around indicating a struggle tells me that he left on his own. Thinking like we would think, what are the odds that any of us would simply sit and wait half a day for a bunch of unknown kids to come help us find the way home?"

"Pretty slim, I would say," Carrie said with a shake of the head. "Any one of us would wait a little while and then start off for home on our own. So what do we do now? Is our job done? We did rescue him from the Indians."

"I don't think so, Sis," I said. "I just have this gut feeling that we need to follow him

110

and make sure he gets home safely. It may be nothing, but since we're here anyway, we might as well make ourselves useful."

Knowing the general details of how to track a person and actually tracking a person, are two entirely different things. I doubt seriously if Samuel was trying to throw anybody off his trail, most likely he was just in a hurry to get home. Nonetheless, with us being as inexperienced at the tracking game as we were, it took us a good while to go very short distances making sure that we were still following him. Time chose not to stand still for us, the sun began to drop toward the horizon just as if it was not concerned about us, and I was really anxious to find him and make sure that he was safe before we bedded down for the night.

We picked up the pace a little bit, and presently we came to a fairly clearly marked trail leading between two low-lying hills. A trail that wide and well-worn had to be in fairly constant use, otherwise nature would have reclaimed it. We didn't really like being that much out in the open, but Samuels tracks had led right to this trail, therefore it would most likely take us right to his home.

And within about ten or fifteen minutes, it did just that.

"Check it out, guys," Carrie said, "the back of a comfy looking little cabin with a corral and a barn. It looks like something off of *Little House on the Prairie*."

And it really did. I could almost imagine in my mind Laura and Mary Ingles going about their daily chores and wondering what mischief Nellie Olson was going to cause next. But reality was a much bigger concern, and it wouldn't be Nellie Olson who tried to scalp us if we made a wrong move.

We watched the house for a little bit from a distance, and when we saw absolutely no movement, we approached it. As we rounded the corner and came to the front of it, my heart skipped a beat. There, lying either dead or unconscious in the front yard, was a frail looking man, and several feet away a couple of busted old timey looking crutches.

Chapter Sixteen

Immediately we threw caution to the wind. I rushed over to the man, knelt beside him, turned him over, and felt for a pulse. He had a nasty knot on the side of his head, and the entire front yard around him look like it had been trampled by buffalo. No doubt that was from a nasty struggle that had taken place.

Almost at once the man's eyes snapped open, and he shouted out a word in utter anguish from the depths of his soul. "SON!"

He looked around at us wildly, his head bobbing back and forth. Knowing that we needed to get him calm and quiet as quickly as possible, I stood up and crouched over, and picked him up in my arms. He probably didn't weigh a hundred and twenty pounds soaking wet; his legs were shriveled to near uselessness from the paralysis.

I carried him inside and laid him on the crude little bed, and without even having to tell her to do so Carrie had immediately rushed over to the well and was drawing out some water for him. Aly was already in the process of building a fire. The man had begun to calm down just a bit, just enough to trade his screaming for crying.

"Ohhhh, my son, my son. I am so sorry, forgive me for not being able to protect you. Curse these wretched and useless legs, curse this weak and worthless back, curse these frail and feeble arms that could not hold you after you had come back to me..."

Aly and I just looked at each other and shook our heads sadly. Carrie rushed in with the water, and we quickly got him to drink some to soothe his thirst and calm his rough and raspy voice. He drank like his stomach was on fire, and when he was done he began to speak again.

"My apologies, children, in my grief I have forgotten my manners. I do not know who you are or from whence you came, but you have my thanks. They left me out there in the yard helpless, knowing that if I were there till

114

nightfall the wild animals of the forest would delight in making a meal out of me. Thank you for finding me, and thank you for bringing me in,"

"We were glad to do so, sir," I said. "But if you please, what happened to Samuel? I think I pretty much have it figured out based on what I've seen out in the yard, but please tell us anyway."

"And how do you know my Samuel?"

"That really doesn't matter much now," I said matter-of-factly, "all that really matters is that you know that God sent us here to help him and you. And I do not mean to be rude, but we have precious little time left to do so. So once again, if you please, what happened here?"

"I have been praying for my son's return for so very long, I had begun to lose hope that it would ever happen. And then just a few hours ago the door burst open and my boy rushed into my arms. It was several moments and a lot of tears on both of our parts before I could get him to explain that God had answered his prayer and sent someone to rescue him. We wept and hugged and wept some more. I felt like I could not possibly ever be so happy again.

"And then I heard it, a low-and menacing voice, 'So, the whelp has made its way back home. What a shame that I must destroy such a tender moment.'

"It was Black Crow. He was standing right in our front door, and behind him was a cadre of warriors. In a flash he was across the room and had snatched my Samuel by the back of the neck and was dragging him out into the yard toward their horses. I cannot use my legs, but I have learned to move about using just my arms and my crutches. Immediately I was up and out the door after them. I would die before I would let them take my son again.

"But I was no match for Black Crow. He took the butt of his knife and in one stroke did the damage that you see to the side of my head. My world went black, I could not see, but I could hear them ride away as I lay crumpled on the ground."

"Is that all?" I asked. "Make sure you have told us absolutely everything, every detail could be crucial if we are to get him back safely."

"It is all, save for one thing. As they rode away Black Crow shouted back to me 'I will have his blood, or the blood of another. If you would like him to live, you are welcome to send another warrior to die in his place.'

"My son is not a warrior," he cried, "nor is there any other 'warrior' to take his place. My son will die tomorrow night, and I can do nothing to stop it."

I looked at the girls, and both of them looked at me. It was very clear that our plan to rescue Samuel was going to have to be drastically altered. Why in the world had it not occurred to me that they had raided his home once, and that they would do so again? Black Crow was not the type to let anything go, nor was he the type to tolerate being embarrassed in front of his warriors. We had tried the rescue route, and it had not worked. All that was left was war.

Chapter Seventeen

Having quickly made some make-shift crutches for the ones that had been broken, we made sure Samuel's father was well set and supplied for a few days, then we made our way out into the woods and went to sleep. We woke up once again in the relative safety of our own time and our hotel room. I'm not certain what emotion first began to course through the girls as they awakened, but for me, it was anger. What right did that bully have to terrorize a little boy and to beat down an old paralyzed father? I was absolutcly, positively, going to beat his face into the ground.

"Easy, big brother," Aly whispered. "If you aren't careful, you will be the fool instead of Black Crow."

She was right, of course. I was angry. Coldly, furiously angry. And though anger is not always a sin, such as when Jesus drove the money changers out of the temple and when Ephesians 4:26 says "Be ye angry, and sin not," unbridled anger such as the type spoken of in Ecclesiastes 7:9 would clearly make me play into Black Crow's hands rather than the other way around. And besides that, I had an entire day to live in our modern time before I would get a shot at him after we went to sleep tonight. I really couldn't afford to be angry for an entire day.

"Guys," I said, "slip down here very quietly, and let's pray. We are going to need it."

And with that, they did, and we did. We prayed that we would have a good day in our time. We prayed that our vehicle would run well. We prayed that God would give our dad clear guidance as to what to preach tonight, and that He would empower him to do so. We prayed for souls to be saved. And above all, we prayed that God would give us the strength and the wisdom and the composure to win this battle and to do so safely. We prayed that it would be Black Crow that became the angry fool rather than me.

Soon we begin to hear our mom and dad stir a bit, and we knew it was time to be up and about our day. After breakfast we headed into town. It was Heritage Day in Rogersville, which is billed as "a celebration of Rogersville's unique heritage." The festival showcases Appalachian music, storytelling, dancers, special events for children, demonstrations of pioneer skills, antique quilts, cars and farm equipment.

It was really cool and helped to take my mind off of my anger. There were musicians playing on hammered dulcimers, experts on the banjo and mandolin and guitar, square dancing, games, and some of the best storytelling you would ever hear. Bearded men in old-timey garb told of the pioneers who first crossed the hills and settled the area. They told of hunters and trappers and traders and of the battles between the white man and the Indians. That last part we were all too familiar with.

We stayed downtown most of the day, ate some phenomenal barbecue from the street vendors, and then went back to the hotel to prepare for the night service. Dad was already studied up and prepared, but there was one more thing he would do to get ready. It was not a surprise to us; we had seen him do it very many times.

"Kids," he called, "you and mom come over here and let's pray together as a family. I am going to need God's help as I preach tonight."

And pray he did. Friends, when my dad prays, it is not a formal connect-the-dots kind of thing. My dad talks to God as if he knows Him personally. It makes me want to be able to pray in the exact same way.

"Dear Lord," he began, "would You please prepare my heart for the meeting and the message to come? Lord, there is nothing that I can do in my flesh that will accomplish anything of any eternal value. If anything real is going to happen, You will have to be the One to do it. Lord, would you please touch these feeble lips of clay? Would You please help me to say all those and only those words which You desire for me to say? Would You please do for me as you did for the disciples at the Last Supper, would you please wash the dust and dirt of the world off of my feet one more time and prepare me for service?

"Lord, would you help my wife and my children to be an active part of the service? Would You please work through them as much as You work through me?

"And Lord, lastly, would You please protect my children as they serve You? Would you be a shield and a hedge of protection about them as they do all of the things that You have called them to do even in their youth? These things we pray in Jesus name, amen."

Now, that last part of my dad's prayer may not have caught you by surprise, but you could have absolutely knocked me over with a feather. I looked over at Aly and Carrie, and they were both wide eyed and open mouthed as well. Did dad know? If not, why would he pray such a thing?

I would have loved to have asked, but what was I going to say? "Hey, Dad, when you prayed that, it made me wonder, do you just by chance know that all of your children go on potentially deadly adventures a lot of nights while we are in these revival meetings?"

No sir, a question like that was not one that I could ask.

Later, though, after the service was over (which, by the way, went extremely well; two more people got saved!) I asked him about his prayer life in general.

"Dad, when you pray, how do you decide what to pray?"

My dad just looked at me with sort of an odd look on his face, and then he answered that question the way he answers almost every question, with Scripture.

"Romans 8:26 says 'Likewise the Spirit also helpeth our infirmities: for we know not what we should pray for as we ought: but the Spirit itself maketh intercession for us with groanings which cannot be uttered.' When I pray, I understand that because I am nothing more than a human, I really don't know how or what to pray. So, in addition to the list of normal things that I pray for, I always try to be very sensitive to the leading of the Holy Spirit in my prayers. Many times I will feel an urging to pray for something or for someone, and I really won't even know why. But if I will follow that inner guidance, I have found that there is always a very good reason for me to pray what the Lord is asking me to pray."

From there dad dropped the subject and went to the counter to order our food. That's my dad, say something incredibly profound one moment and order a Big Mac the next.

Chapter Eighteen

We had stayed up pretty late to fellowship, since this would be our last night in Rogersville for a while. But finally we had gotten back to the hotel and gotten bedded down for the night. I was as tense as a violin string, but with all of the praying and preaching and thinking during the day, I felt pretty certain that I was in control of my anger rather than my anger being in control of me.

And that helped me to get to sleep pretty quickly.

"Good morning, young man," the Conductor said pleasantly. "If you like, you may have the privilege of awakening your sisters for a change."

Sure enough, Carrie and Aly were both sound asleep in the bottom of the boat.

"Hey, Rip Van Winklets," I said, "why don't you two wake up and join us?"

The girls yawned and stretched, and then both sat straight up in the boat at the same time.

"What are we going to do?" Aly nearly shouted. "Black Crow has Samuel, his dad is paralyzed, and now he doubtless knows about us as well. Do you think we can slip him out of there again?"

"No, I..."

But Aly was wound up tight, and she interrupted me without thinking.

"I brought the Vaseline, sparklers, and Tabasco that I didn't get to use in West Virginia!"

As before, I just shook my head, not even having the faintest guess as to what plan she had formulated with that mixture of ingredients, but somehow knowing that it would be absolutely epic.

"No, Sis, you just hold on to those for another time. I think slipping Samuel out unnoticed again will be absolutely impossible, no matter what distractions you cause. If we are going to get Samuel out, we're going to have to use the formula that Black Crow himself laid out for us."

Aly just looked at me, confused. But I could tell from the way Carrie dropped her head and shook it slowly back and forth that she knew exactly what I meant.

"You are going to fight in his place," she said. "You are going to sacrifice yourself for him."

Aly's eyes got wider than I had ever seen them, and she started to speak but I cut her off.

"I am going to fight in his place, but let's hold back on that talk of a sacrifice just yet. Philippians 4:13 says 'I can do all things through Christ which strengtheneth me.' We are just going to have to trust that the God who allowed David to defeat Goliath can enable me to defeat Black Crow. Besides, the odds on me against him aren't nearly as steep as the odds that David faced versus Goliath."

"But he is a trained warrior, and you are not," the Conductor said grimly.

"And that is exactly what Saul said to David," I said as I smiled up at him.

"Yes, yes it is," he said, "and yet with one smooth, white rock, the giant became small, and the small became a giant."

"Begging your pardon, sir," Carrie asked, "but the Bible doesn't say what color the rock was, but you very clearly and without any hesitation called it a white rock."

"Did I?" He said. "I suppose I must remember to be a little more careful around someone as observant as yourself."

And then he changed the subject and for some reason none of us had any desire to push him on it any farther. We discussed it later and came to even more conclusions about our mysterious friend.

After a while we drew close to the point of the river at which we would disembark.

"Where would you like me to put you ashore today?" The Conductor asked, "Upstream as yesterday?"

"No, sir," I said, "put us off at the point of the river that is nearest to the Indian encampment. There will be no need for subtlety anymore, nor would it be effective if we tried to use it."

A few moments later we were standing ashore, the Conductor had bid us a fond farewell, and we were alone.

There really was no rush. We knew that the "battle" if it could be so-called, would not take place until right at sundown. My plan was to arrive a half an hour or so before that time, and offer myself as the one to fight in Samuel's place.

We spent the bulk of the day right there by the riverside. I had brought along some fishing line and hooks, and we made some makeshift fishing poles from tree branches that we cut off of trees near the river. We dug some grubs out of the ground, and after a couple of hours of fishing had a nice stringer full of smallmouth bass.

"Let's pack everything up and get ready to go," I said. "I want to get to the campsite a little earlier than we had planned."

"Why?" Aly asked. "Are you anxious to die just a few minutes earlier?"

"Thanks for the encouragement, pipsqueak," I said, "but I don't plan on dying at all, or at least not today. It is actually this stringer of fish that makes me want to go a little bit earlier."

Carrie and Aly just blinked their eyes and shook their heads at that, but they let it go. It didn't take us long to be on the move, and we took a leisurely pace as we went. I walked, and I prayed; I prayed, and I walked. I was a pretty good fighter, I knew that, but this was not a game to Black Crow.

An hour or so before sundown, we simply and boldly strode right into the center of the camp.

Chapter Nineteen

It seemed to catch all of the Indians off guard for three white children to calmly walk into their midst. But only for a second. When they had regained their composure, we immediately found ourselves encircled by nasty, sharp looking spear points. If a person wanted to become a piece of Swiss cheese, making any sudden movement right then would definitely be the way to do it. The Indians were chattering to each other excitedly in the language that they understood and that we did not.

Suddenly, they all fell quiet and parted from side to side, though never pointing their spears away from us.

And there, walking calmly and slowly through their midst, was the old chief, followed by his two sons.

The chief stopped in front of me and stared at me with penetrating gray eyes.

"Hail, great chief of the Creek Indians," I said. And then I stretched out my stringer of fish and handed it to him.

"I bring a gift, a token of peace from my people to yours."

Suddenly, a harsh voice snapped me and everyone else to attention.

"And what do you know of peace," Black Crow said with a sneer. "Your people are thieves and liars and murderers. I will kill you where you stand!"

"My son!" the chief said in a low yet commanding voice. "Visitors to our midst will be allowed to speak, and none will be killed except by fair battle or by my command."

"Thank you, kind chief," I said. "Truly, many of my people are thieves and liars and murders as your son has said. But my people are as varied in their beliefs and behavior as are yours. Many Indian tribes are every bit the thieves and liars and murderers as many of the white men are. Skin does not determine behavior or character, those things are determined by the heart, the spirit."

"You have wisdom beyond your years, young one," the chief said. "What brings you into our midst bearing gifts on this day?"

"I come on behalf of the boy, Samuel. I wish for him to be released and sent home to his ailing father."

"He will be released only by his death," Black Crow shouted. "It was I who captured him, it was I who recaptured him, and none but I may set him free."

I looked over the chief, and he nodded his head slowly up and down as the feathers of his headdress made the motion seemed even more emphatic.

"My son speaks the truth," he said, "by the custom of our people he may not be released unless my son chooses to do so."

"And I do not," Black Crow said with sadistic glee, "for tonight I shall slay him in battle, and then I shall be the chief of this tribe in place of my father."

"Will a dishonest young man truly be made the chief of such a great tribe?"

As soon as I said it, things happened as fast as a lightning strike. Two warriors were behind me pressing against my back, Black

Crow was nose to nose with me, and I could feel his blade against my neck.

"Who dares call Black Crow a liar? Speak quickly, before I move my hand but a little and end your life."

"Did you or did you not tell the boy's father that another warrior could take his place and fight in his stead?"

At that, Black Crow stepped back, his eyes grew wide, and suddenly he erupted in peals of hateful laughter.

"And where is the warrior that would take his place? All I see before me is a boy dressed in strange clothes; I see no warrior at all."

I really had not thought of that before that moment. Though I was bigger than Samuel and physically about the same size as Black Crow, when he looked at me he did not see a young man of the wilderness. He saw an oddity, someone that he had no reason to respect.

It is at times like that I have learned to thank God for the trials in my life. How many times has something frightening or unpleasant happened, and I have realized later that it was designed by God for a specific purpose? There is an old song that says, "God Already Knew," and buddy, God really did already know!

"You see no warrior?" I asked slowly. "Then why are the rattles on the leather strap around your neck so much smaller than mine," I said as I pulled the rattles from our dead rattlesnake out of my pocket.

The warriors who were gathered around open their eyes wide with amazement. To kill a snake as huge as the one that had been the owner of the rattle in my hand was a very rare thing. Every warrior there was wearing a rattle around his neck, including the chief himself, and not one of them was half as big as the one that I was holding in my hand.

"It means nothing," Black Crow said as he tried to regain the upper hand.

"Are you afraid, then?" I said with an intentional sneer. "Perhaps it is I that do not see a warrior present. Perhaps I should offer to fight your brother; it seems as though he must have far more courage than you."

That did the trick. Oh boy, did that ever do the trick! Black Crow exploded in a fit of anger and lunged at me with the knife. But one word of command from his father stopped the knife in mid-air, thankfully for me.

"CEASE, my son. If it is a battle that you desire, then you will honor our customs and ways as you do that battle. A warrior has stepped forward to take the place of the one you have captured. Will you fight him, or will they both go free?"

I have to admit that at that moment I was secretly praying and thinking "both go free, both go free, both go free, both go free!" But naturally, it was not going to be that easy...

Chapter Twenty

Night had fallen. The fire in the center of the camp was casting eerie shadows all about. Carrie and Aly and Samuel and I were in the teepee that had been provided for us. In just a matter of moments, I was going to be in a fight for my life and for Samuel's.

"Don't do it, Kyle, please don't do it," Carrie said. "Let's just open the teepee door and all four of us just run as fast as we possibly can."

"That wouldn't work, Sis. We would get about a tenth of a mile before those warriors on horseback caught up with us. And even if we were to escape, where would that leave

Samuel? Once we were gone, it would be him instead of me."

"Then please let it be that way," Samuel said. "You three just run away and let me face this. I know Jesus as my Savior; I'm ready to go, and tonight is just as good a night as any."

I just looked at that precious kid and smiled. He was braver than those Indians out there knew; they could stand to learn a few things from him.

"No, we are not going to do that. We know the same Jesus that you know. He gave Himself for us, and if need be, I will give myself for you. But let's not assume that I'm going to lose, okay? This isn't my first rodeo, and I'm batting a thousand so far."

Samuel just looked at me with scrunched up eyes, not comprehending my baseball analogy. I waved it off with my hand, and said, "What we do need to do is pray. And now, we have four voices praying instead of just three. I figure that ups our small odds significantly!"

"Actually, Bro, if you count dad's prayer last night, and mom surely was praying the same thing as he did, you have six voices praying."

"Well, by George, I do believe you're right," I said with a smile.

And we prayed. We prayed hard. We prayed that just as God had given David victory, He would do the same for me. But we didn't stop there. We also prayed that God would somehow bring peace between the Indians and the white man. We prayed that people who knew the Lord among our people would take the gospel to their people. We prayed that not only would the bloodshed cease, but the blood of Jesus would be applied to hearts, and that white man and Indians would find themselves hand-in-hand worshipping the Lord Jesus Christ together.

When we had finished praying, I looked up and saw a young warrior standing in the teepee door. How long he had been standing there I do not know, but I noticed that he had his head reverently bowed until a second or two after we finished our prayer and then looked up.

"It is time, White Warrior. And may the God who has given you such courage grant that you may fight bravely on this night."

There was nothing left to do but do it, so we all got to our feet and followed the warrior into the center of the camp. The drums were beating loudly and rythmatically. The sparks from the fire were illuminating the night sky, and the moon up above seemed to be nearly blood red. Every teepee was emptied, and every man, woman, and child with red skin was standing in a circle around the center of the camp watching as Black Crow danced and gyrated wildly.

He was definitely athletic. He moved with the grace of a ballet dancer, jumped like a basketball star, and had plenty of muscle but little to no body fat on his lean frame.

Carrie leaned over into my ear and shouted, but with the cacophony of noise it sound a lot like a whisper.

"You be careful, big brother, that's not some overweight miner you're dealing with."

"Got it, Sis, got it."

With three loud thuds, the music and dancing immediately stopped.

"My people," Black Crow shouted, "tonight I shall prove my worth as the next chief of this tribe. For too long the white man has terrorized our people. Now, a warrior from among them has stepped forth to challenge me. What I do to him, I shall do to them all, as you follow me into battle!"

He positively shouted that last phrase, and immediately every warrior and child in the camp joined him in that bloodcurdling scream of hatred and anger.

When the noise stopped, I began to prepare myself to fight. What came next was a shock that I had not anticipated.

"You may now choose the weapons with which we shall fight, White Warrior."

Chapter Twenty-One

Weapons! I was expecting a good old fashion hand and fist kind of fight! I have never fought with a weapon of any kind in my life.

"Um," I began to stammer, "I normally fight with my fists."

And instantly the laughter was directed toward me. From every corner it came, peals of ringing laughter tinged with hatred and disbelief.

"Do weapons frighten you?" Black Crow sneered. "They do not frighten me or my people. Death itself does not frighten us. Are you frightened, then? Do you wish to withdraw? Shall I kill the other white warrior in your place?"

Man, what a bind. When a person does not know how to fight with a weapon, the weapon becomes dangerous to only one person–himself. I knew that, but I also knew that I could not back down now, and that I somehow had to regain the upper hand in everyone's mind.

"Frightened?" I said as I laughed a confident laugh that did not mirror how I actually felt inside. "No, it is you who should be frightened, since it is you who are about to lose a battle to an unarmed warrior."

Man, did that turn things around. Every eye in the camp grew wide and looked at Black Crow. How would he respond to such taunting?

"You may remain empty-handed if you wish," he said angrily, "but I shall not. Since you refuse to choose your weapon, I shall choose."

And then he slowly and dramatically drew that knife out of that sheath, the very same knife the trader had brought him that sliced through hardwoods like soft butter...

Chapter Twenty-Two

Hey, this is Carrie. Since Kyle was obviously a bit tied up at the moment, I will take the story from here. When Black Crow pulled that knife out, everyone in the camp including the chief stepped back to a respectable distance. Everything was absolutely dead quiet. Kyle dropped back one leg and put both hands up in a defensive position, and the bulk of his weight was on his back leg to allow him easy and quick movement, and also the ability to use the kicks that our dad had taught him.

And then they both began to move slowly, feeling each other out. Tears of fear were streaming down Aly's face. Mine too.

Kyle and Black Crow circled each other warily. I knew my brother was strong, really strong, but that knife in Black Crow's hand was gleaming and razor sharp. Everything was at stake for him; if Kyle won, he would never be chief. That being the case, Black Crow would not hesitate to kill...

Suddenly he lunged. He shot out the knife straight ahead of him in a jabbing motion, and Kyle deftly sidestepped it to the right. As he did, he immediately fired a quick jab with his right hand that glanced off of Black Crow's forehead. It was not nearly as clean a shot as I was used to seeing from my brother, but then again, he had never fought anybody holding a knife either.

Black Crow staggered back just a little bit and shook his head in surprise. I'm guessing that is the first time he had ever been hit. Angrily he growled and took a wider stance, still circling, but much more warily than before.

For his part, Kyle had a look on his face of absolute calm and peace. If I didn't know better, it would look to me like he was sitting peacefully under a tree somewhere reading a book! And that seemed to anger Black Crow all the more. Once more he lunged, and this time Kyle sidestepped to the left, and fired a strong and quick left jab. That one rang true, and everyone in the camp heard the loud "thwap" as it made contact just below Black Crow's right eye.

"Is that the best you can do?" Kyle asked as if he was bored. "Maybe you should get a bigger weapon, say, a spear or something. Or I know, maybe you should just have someone else fight for you, since you clearly don't know what you're doing."

Black Crow's eyes got wide like saucers, he screamed a guttural scream of hatred, and swung the knife across his body from left to right trying to take Kyle's head off with one swipe.

That movement was dramatic, but going across your body and then coming back the other way is something that you cannot help but telegraph. Black Crow's anger had made him careless, just as Kyle hoped. Kyle saw it coming a mile away, ducked under it and then fired an uppercut into Black Crow's ribs.

We heard a loud "crack," and I knew that my muscular big brother had broken a couple of ribs for a knife wielding bully. In complete control now, Kyle looped his right arm around Black Crow's neck, stepped behind and past him with his right leg, then twisted his body and swept Black Crow completely off his feet. He landed flat on his back with a loud thud, and we could hear all of the wind go out of him. Kyle immediately yanked the knife out of his hand and placed it against his throat. Black Crow just lay there, gasping and defeated, looking up at my brother, and knowing that his own life was about to end.

"His life is yours to take, White Warrior," the voice of the chief said stoically.

Kyle didn't even hesitate. He stood up quickly, whirled, and performed a carbon-copy throw of what Black Crow had done a couple of days earlier. The knife sunk into an oak tree at the edge of camp, all the way to the hilt. I did not know my brother could do that!

"His life is not mine to take. Our God gave him life, and I will not willingly take from Him what does not belong to me. I did not come to shed more blood; I came to stop more blood from being shed, the blood of the white man and the blood of the Indian. All of our blood came from the same father, Adam, so all of us are family. You bleed red, I bleed red as well. But if I have my way, all of us will keep all of our blood on this night."

The old chief stared silently at Kyle for what seemed to be an eternity.

"You are both wise and kind, White Warrior."

"He is weak!" Black Crow spat as he stood up, clutching his ribs with one arm. He pointed his finger at Kyle and screamed, "He was too weak to kill when he had the chance! When I am chief, I shall hunt him down and take his filthy scalp!"

"No, my son, you will not," the old chief said firmly, "for you shall not be chief. The White Warrior has taught me much by his spirit. He speaks truth. Enough blood has been shed. From this day forward, we will seek peace and fight only when attacked. You will not be able to lead my people in that manner, but Falling Rain will.

"Hear me, my people!" he shouted. "It is my decree that from this day forward, Falling Rain shall be chief of the Creek peoples!"

That was too much for Black Crow to take. He lunged at his brother, ready to kill him...and was immediately surrounded by all of the same razor-sharp spears we ourselves had been surrounded by earlier.

"You may choose, my brother," Falling Rain said calmly.

Black Crow hung his head in defeat. It was then that we knew our mission was finished, and that Samuel, and a whole lot more folks that God loves and died for, would be just fine.

Coming Soon

The Night Heroes Book Five

Ghost Ship

The heavy mist hung in the air like a shroud, blinding us to what we needed to see. I wondered if she was still there or had perhaps put silently out to sea for some reason. But the next breeze that blew reminded me how foolish that notion was. When the mist parted for briefest of times, there she was, black sails still hanging, the ghost ship that the people for miles around feared as if she was death itself.

"What now, big brother?" Carrie asked with a tinge of fear.

"We really don't have much of an option left to us, now do we?" I answered matter-of-factly. "I have to get aboard that ship."

Meet the Author

Dr. Wagner is the founder and pastor of Cornerstone Baptist Church of Mooresboro, North Carolina. He was saved in 1979 and began preaching regularly as a twelve-year-old boy in 1982.

He earned an Associate's Degree in Communications Technology from Cleveland Community College in 1989. He earned his Bachelor's Degree in Pastoral Studies with highest honors in 1997 and then his Master's and Doctorate with highest honors from Carolina Bible College in 2001 and 2003. He founded Cornerstone Baptist Church in 1997. He has been teaching at the Carolina Bible College since 2000 and has been a professor since 2003.

He has been writing books since 2009, with Cry from the Coal Mine being his first fiction book.

Along with pastoring, Dr. Wagner preaches in many revivals, camp meetings, and family conferences each year.

He married Dana in 1994. They have three children: Caleb, Karis, and Aléthia.

Other Books in the Night Heroes Series